GLIMMER OF DEATH

OTHER REALM, BOOK 3

BY HEATHER G HARRIS

DEDICATION

For my children, I'd do anything for you.
Love you now and always.

CHAPTER 1

M Y BEST FRIEND is dying. I've been in denial these last three weeks, but now I have to face it. The slow beep of the machine is driving me mad. It shouldn't be so slow. She shouldn't be so lifeless. Lucy is a warm caring girl, always up for a laugh and a dance. She's vibrant and fun; she should not be dying in a hospice while the uncaring machine beeps on.

The nurse came by a few minutes ago and told us that it wouldn't be long now. Lucy's family are in shock. We kept her condition from them for as long as we could. I'd been hoping for a miracle. Lucy had been hoping it was all a terrible mistake.

I couldn't explain to Lucy that her supposed boyfriend had condemned her to death. I couldn't explain that he was an incubus who had broken the rules and fed on her one too many times. Her organs were shutting down, her life was ending, all because of one greedy little shit. I railed against it. I screamed at the unfairness of losing my best friend after I'd already lost so much. I couldn't lose Lucy. I just couldn't.

Lucy's parents were shattered and bewildered. A week ago they hadn't even known she was sick; now she was a day or two away from dying. The doctors thought it was an autoimmune disease. I knew better.

When Gato and I went to Lucy's house after the Ronan debacle, she was already tired. It hadn't taken much convincing to get her to the doctors. They'd been concerned rather than alarmed, but I'd been alarmed enough for everyone even though I was trying to play it cool.

I convinced Lucy to let me pay for a barrage of private tests, and I got her seen the next day. The tests came back quickly and conclusively: she had multiple organ failure, and – worse still – her digestive system was shutting down. The doctor explained sympathetically and kindly that you can only survive a matter of weeks once that happens. The organ failure, plus the digestive system failure, meant her condition was fatal. Lucy only had a little time left, three or four weeks at most.

Lucy had beamed brightly and thanked the doctor for taking the time to explain it so thoroughly. She walked out of the hospital and paid my parking ticket like everything was fine.

'Lucy…' I started.

'Not yet, Jess,' she said calmly. 'We have things to do.'

It turned out her things to do were horribly practical. We went to an undertaker's and planned and paid for her funeral. She picked the songs she wanted to be played when we walked out of the church. She picked the music for when she was to be interred. She chose her flowers. Then we went to a local hotel and asked about the cost of a wake.

Next, we went to a solicitor's office. Lucy gave her instructions with clear eyes and a steady, even voice. I tried to excuse myself to give her some privacy but she objected, holding my hand in a vice-like grip. I stayed.

We remained in the solicitor's reception room while her will was drawn up. She had split her assets between her parents and her brother. She left me her jewellery. Every minute killed me a little more.

I wasn't responsible for her illness but I felt like I was. It was *my* realm that had inflicted this on her, a realm she had no idea about. The Verdict bound me, and I couldn't even tell her that her 'boyfriend' James was responsible for her dying.

They had only been on a few dates, seven or eight at most. He didn't answer when she rang, so she left him a voicemail saying that she was very sick. He never called back. I'd kill him if I got the chance, and I wouldn't even feel slightly bad about it. He wouldn't be the first person I've killed.

After the longest day in the world, Lucy and I curled up on the sofa and finally she cried. Gato placed his giant head in her lap and whined.

'I'm scared, Jess,' she confessed.

My internal radar pinged *true,* and it just about broke me. 'It's going to be okay,' I said helplessly. *Lie.*

Lucy didn't reply. She didn't need my truth-seeking abilities to know I was lying. We cuddled together until the sun came up, talking quietly about anything but the fact that she was dying. We didn't sleep a wink that night, nor a lot of the nights that followed. Gato spent each night on Lucy's bed, and each day he was drained and tired. He slept more than ever. He was helping, keeping her alive, giving her the gift of as much time as he could, but it was costing him dearly.

Lucy quit her job and I bailed on my business. I left Hes to re-direct new enquiries and turned on my out-of-hours email response. If I only had days left with Lucy, I wasn't going to waste them.

She found an article that said purple fruit boosted your immune system. She ate purple grapes, aubergines and purple cabbage. Another article suggested Roquefort cheese helped, so Lucy ate some of that with the purple grapes. When you're desperate, you'll do anything, anything to give you five minutes of hope.

I called everyone and anyone from the Other realm who might help. First I called Wilf, but he explained that he couldn't change her. The Connection strictly regulates the conversion of humans to wolves; they can only be changed if they're going to die immediately and through

4

unnatural causes. Lucy's illness, although triggered by an incubus, was natural. Her organs were just failing.

I called Amber DeLea, Nate and Emory. Amber didn't make promises; she told me flatly that there was no witch or wizard, potion, spell or rune that could help us. Then she hung up. She didn't send an invoice for her advice, though, which was positively caring for Amber. Nate explained that Lucy couldn't be turned. A vampyr's organs have to be shut down carefully for them to survive the transition, and it was too late for Lucy.

Emory gently explained that dragons were born, but he promised he'd consult with the dragon Elders and their archives to see if anything could be done to help Lucy. He kept his word, phoning me every day with updates. I knew he was doing his best and trying to give me hope, but the chances of finding something were slim.

How could we have a whole realm full of magic and not be able to save one person?

Emory's brethren dropped some books around for me every day, and every night I read them under cover of darkness. If Lucy had seen them they would have appeared like normal books to her, but she would have had zero inclination to pick them up and look at them. The Other realm protected itself from discovery in a myriad of ways. I couldn't care less about the Other realm's secrecy. I just wanted it to *help*.

I called Leo Harfen and the elves. I called Joyce and

the dryads. Emory got me contact details for other species, too. I even called the trolls and spoke to the Elders after being on hold for literally an entire day. I called the merman, Jack Fairglass. No one could help me. No one could help Lucy.

Let me tell you, there is no despair so absolute as the terminal diagnosis of a loved one. You start grieving at that moment and you don't stop. They are still alive and you're already mourning their loss. My parents' deaths had been a swift and sudden shock, and it had been hard to accept, but this was worse – the waiting for death to take her, the inevitability and the helplessness.

When Lucy and I whispered wistfully to each other and promised that we'd make the most of the time we had left, it felt empty and hollow. We both knew it.

We ate lobster. We swam in the sea. We took a nude painting class. We did whatever Lucy wanted. And time kept marching on. It slipped through my fingers while I clung to it desperately.

Her condition worsened quickly. I went with her to tell her parents that she was dying. The moment they opened the door they could tell that something was terribly wrong. Lucy's smile was wan and her normally pale skin was ashen. She had bags under her eyes and she had lost weight she could ill afford to lose.

Her mum, Sandy, instantly took her into her arms. 'What's wrong, baby girl?' she asked.

Lucy started to cry. 'I'm dying, Mum. I'm dying.'

Suffice to say there were a lot of tears, an ocean of them. Her parents tried to hope, to suggest that there was more to be done, but there wasn't. We'd tried everything.

There was guilt there, too. Lucy was adopted; perhaps her birth parents would have known what was wrong with her. Perhaps it was a genetic condition. Perhaps, perhaps, perhaps... So much guilt and desperation. We were drowning in it. Sandy dug up the adoption papers and scoured through Lucy's medical history but there was nothing to help. As I'd known there wouldn't be.

Four days later, Lucy was so exhausted that she couldn't get out of bed to wash or use the bathroom. She was conscious enough to make the call that it was time for the hospice. There would be no hospital because there was no point – she needed end-of-life care, not treatment.

The hospice made arrangements to send a car to pick her up. I left Gato at her house. Dogs were allowed there at limited times if it was pre-arranged. I would take him to see Lucy another day, but he needed rest as much as she did.

Lucy had only been in the hospice three days when they told us the end was coming. It wasn't imminent, but it would be soon. Her parents went home to shower and pack an overnight bag. From now on, they wouldn't be leaving her side. Her brother did the same.

I stayed. Listening to the beeping.

I leaned over Lucy and kissed her. 'I don't know if you can hear me, Luce, but if you can, don't be afraid. I'm doing this to help you, to give you a chance.' I squeezed her. Then I picked up my leather jacket and turned out the overhead lights. I turned on a lamp, casting shadows across the room. I left her, alone and dying in the dark.

I slung on my jacket and sat in the waiting room. I fiddled with Emory's emerald pendant around my neck, moving it left and then right, left and then right. It was a nervous habit I'd developed these last few weeks. Irritated, I pulled my hand away from my necklace; it wasn't a safety blanket, it was just metal and rock.

I checked the time anxiously: 6:45 p.m. I hauled out my phone and called Nate. Phones weren't allowed in the waiting room but I wasn't letting Lucy's door out of my sight. I needed to know who entered it, and when.

My phone rang only once before it was picked up. 'Hi, Jinx,' Nate answered.

'I need you. Now. Can you come?'

There was a heavy pause. 'I've told you, Jinx. I'm sorry, but we can't turn Lucy. She won't survive it. We can only turn healthy people.'

'I know, I know. Just come, okay?'

'I'm in London. I'll be an hour,' he said finally.

'Bring Gato,' I ordered. I hung up without saying anything more. Now I just had to wait.

CHAPTER 2

F OR THE NEXT hour I diligently watched Lucy's door. Crafting my alibi, I made plenty of eye contact with the staff as they went about their business. At 7:40 p.m., the nurse went into Lucy's room. I heard her gasp before she ran out straight to the sister on the desk. They whispered together urgently, gesturing and hissing. The sister stood up.

I made my way over, gathering my intention. 'Is everything all right?' I asked innocently.

When they turned to me, I released my intention. 'Clear,' I intoned and then, 'Replace.' I wiped their memories of Lucy being gone without them noticing and replaced it with an understanding that she'd been picked up by an elite hospital in Switzerland for experimental treatment. There really was a clinic in Switzerland, The Hoppas Centre. Lucy and I had applied there the first week after her diagnosis but we'd been knocked back.

Another nurse approached. 'Is everything all right?' She repeated my words.

'Lucy has been taken to the Hoppas Centre in Switzerland. For experimental treatment,' I explained. My internal radar pinged. *Lie.*

The sister and the other nurse nodded their agreement, their eyes still a little glassy and unfocused. The newcomer frowned. 'It's too late for that. She needs to be here, to be comfortable and treated with dignity.' *True.*

'It was her choice. If a spot opened, she wanted to take it,' I said firmly. 'I don't think she even told her family she'd applied. She didn't want to give them false hope.'

'Which this undoubtedly will,' the nurse griped.

I glared at her. 'We all need hope.'

She opened her mouth but the sister reached over and touched her arm. The nurse shut her mouth with a clack, turned on her heel and walked away. She didn't like it, but she didn't have to. She just had to *believe* it.

I cleared my throat. 'I guess I'd better go and shower. I'll call and let you know once I've heard from the clinic that she's arrived. Can you tell her family for me?'

The sister raised an eyebrow but nodded. I made my excuses and left.

I went out to the darkened car park and looked around. My car was gone. I could feel Nate was getting closer; he was nearly here. A few moments later a black Ford Explorer pulled in and I knew it was him. I headed towards it and opened the boot. Gato stood and gave me a lick. I eyed him with concern.

'Are you okay, boy?' I asked, giving him a full body cuddle. He licked me again in response and gave a little wag. He did seem a lot brighter. With Lucy in the hospice he'd had a few days recovery, though she'd deteriorated rapidly without him. 'Thank you for trying to save her,' I said, looking into his soulful eyes. He hooked his head over my shoulder in a hug and I hugged him back. 'Do you have energy enough to send us to the Third? Just an hour.'

Gato gave an affirmative bark.

Nate had unbuckled his seat back and was waiting unobtrusively for us to finish. 'The Third?' he queried. Nate only had one triangle on his head so I couldn't explain without breaking the Verdict.

'I'll tell you later,' I said. Once he'd been to the Third with me, I wouldn't *technically* be breaking the Verdict because he would have experienced it. Pure sophistry on my part; I was skating on thin ice, but I would do anything to help Lucy.

I put a collar and a lead on Gato. It was dog visiting time, so he wouldn't stick out. Pets As Therapy dogs were often used in places like this. I turned to Nate. 'The shadow thing you can do – can you take someone with you?'

He was silent for a moment. 'Yes,' he said finally. 'But only short distances.'

'That's all we need.' I turned to my hound. It was 7:50

p.m. 'One hour,' I instructed. I reached out and grabbed Nate's hand. Gato jumped at me and touched his snout to my forehead. The sky lightened slightly.

I checked the time, 6:50 p.m. Perfect. 'Thanks, boy.'

I walked into the hospice confidently. Nothing to see here, just another therapy dog coming for a visit. The security guy's eyes slid over us.

I led us up the stairs to the other side of the building until we were near the waiting room. En route, I noticed many areas of shadow; I created more by switching off a few lights. At the waiting room, I peeked carefully around the corner. Sure enough, there was the other me sitting staring at Lucy's door.

Nate stared at the second me, his eyes wild. 'Later,' I promised.

There was a toilet next to us. I reached in and turned off the light. 'That's Lucy's room.' I pointed to the door that the other me was fixated on. 'Can you do your shadow thing from there to here?' I nodded at the darkened toilet.

'It's called phasing. And yes.'

'Do it then. Go and disconnect all of Lucy's monitors. You'll need to turn them off so they don't flatline when she's gone. Then bring Lucy here. Oh, and grab her phone off the bedside table.'

Nate gave me a long look, but he walked into the darkened toilet and disappeared. It seemed like ages but it must have only been a couple of minutes before he was back with an unconscious Lucy in his arms.

'Phase back all the way to the car park,' I instructed. 'We'll take my car.'

He nodded and disappeared again.

Gato and I walked casually through the hospice. We had one small stop to make on the way out. It had taken me three days to find this door marked *Security* in very small letters. I knocked firmly and gathered my intention.

The door opened and an aged security guard looked out at me with cynical eyes, 'How can I help you, Miss?'

Ugh, by not calling me 'Miss'. I released my intention, 'By wiping the last two hours of security footage and logs, and then forgetting that you did it. And forgetting you saw me, too.'

The old man swayed, and I had a moment of alarm. Then he steadied. 'Right you are.' He shut the door in my face and hopefully went to do as I'd asked – okay, compelled. I didn't feel good about messing with people's minds, but I'd do anything to save Lucy.

Gato and I continued towards the exit. We were nearly out of the building when I heard a shout. 'Hey!' one of the security guys called. My heart hammering, I turned to him and gathered my intention. 'What breed is he?' he asked pointing to Gato.

Hell hound. 'Great Dane,' I replied. *Lie.* I gave a friendly smile and a wave and kept on walking, letting my intention fizzle out. Damn, this was tense.

I walked through the shadowy car park to my trusty black Ford Focus. Nate was standing next to it with Lucy in his arms. I looked dubiously at my companions; it was going to be a tight fit. 'Put Lucy in the front with me,' I told Nate. 'You'll have to squish in the back with Gato.'

He did as I asked and buckled Lucy carefully into the front seat before climbing in the back. Lucy sagged and her head rolled back. She looked pale and lifeless, and it terrified me.

The boot was too small for Gato even if I removed the parcel shelf, so he climbed into the back seat. He turned around twice in the confined space before settling down with his head and forepaws on Nate's lap.

As I started the car engine and drove calmly out of the car park, I dialled a number from memory.

'Jinx?'

'Are you home?' I asked abruptly.

'Yes,' he affirmed.

'I'm on my way. See you in twenty.' I rang off. It was time for a miracle. I wouldn't settle for anything less.

CHAPTER 3

I PARKED UP at Wilf's mansion and we all climbed out
of the car. When I rang the doorbell, Mrs Dawes
opened it with her usual exuberance. That faltered a little
when she saw a vampyr carrying an unconscious woman
in his arms.

She blinked twice. 'I'm sorry,' she said to Nate. 'Lord
Samuel doesn't allow vampyrs permission to enter his
family home.'

Nate nodded calmly, clearly used to it.

'I'll carry the girl,' Mrs Dawes offered. She came
down the steps and lifted Lucy easily into her arms. Mrs
Dawes was a shifter, of course, but I was still surprised at
her strength. Even with all of her weight loss, Lucy must
still have been nearly fifty kilograms.

I wasn't sure if vampyrs got cold, but I chucked Nate
my car keys just in case. He could sit in the car with the
heater and radio on. He caught the keys easily. 'I doubt
I'll be too long,' I said.

Nate gave me an undecipherable look and returned to
the car. He sat in the front seat this time, ready to make a

speedy exit if it was needed. I appreciated his forethought but I hoped it wouldn't be necessary.

I followed Mrs Dawes into Wilf's mansion, shutting the heavy front door behind us since Mrs Dawes' arms were otherwise occupied. She strode through the corridor easily, showing no signs of strain from carrying her burden.

When we walked into the main reception room, the overhead lights were off and lamps were lit around the room. The fire was raging in the fireplace. The ambience was warm and friendly. Wilf was alone in the huge room, reclining with a book on one of the sofas. He put the book down and quirked an eyebrow at the sight of an unconscious Lucy. 'Set her down over here,' he ordered Mrs Dawes, gesturing to the sofa next to him.

Mrs Dawes laid Lucy down gently. She hadn't stirred once in her journey from the hospice.

'Leave us,' Wilf instructed Mrs Dawes.

The housekeeper opened her mouth, presumably to object, but then closed it and left, shutting the door behind her.

'She's dying,' I said, stating the obvious.

Wilf nodded solemnly. 'Yes.'

'She's my best friend. She's my family. She's all I have left. You saved Mrs Dawes. Save her.'

'It's against the rules of the Connection.' His tone was final though tinged with regret.

'Archie said you can do it in extreme conditions, like if someone is dying. Lucy is dying.'

'Of natural causes,' Wilf replied calmly, regretfully. 'She isn't dying through violence.'

'This wasn't natural!' I objected, fists clenched, 'An incubus did this to her.'

'She's human. She isn't of the Other.'

'The Other has condemned her,' I argued. 'The Other owes her.'

'The laws are clear,' Wilf continued gently. 'She has to be dying from violent means.' *True.*

'You saved Mrs Dawes – Archie told me you did. She was sick, just like Lucy.'

Wilf sighed. 'She'd been poisoned, so it wasn't a natural illness that was killing her. It was a particularly violent poison at that.'

'That's splitting hairs!' I shouted in frustration. 'You have to help me!' I stepped closer to Lucy and Wilf stepped back, closer to the fire to give me some space.

My hands were shaking. God, I really didn't want to do what I needed to do. I leaned down and kissed Lucy's forehead. 'I'm so sorry,' I whispered to her.

I reached into my leather jacket pocket. It had been empty before but now it was not. Now Glimmer sat in it, unwrapped and ready. Of course it was; Glimmer was always up for mayhem.

With a rock in my throat and unsteady hands, I

pulled it out of my pocket. Wilf watched me, steadily, but I thought I caught an approving look in his eye. Loopholes: they were my last hope.

I relaxed my hold on Glimmer and let it do its thing. It sang as it sliced into Lucy's flesh, ripping her from neck to navel. Blood sprayed everywhere. I was covered in it. Hot blood. Lucy's blood.

I dropped Glimmer to the floor with nerveless hands and suddenly I couldn't see through my tears. 'Save her,' I sobbed to Wilf. 'Please save her.'

He let out an animalistic growl. 'You will owe the pack, Jessica Sharp.' There was something formulaic and formal in his tone. It was more than a passing phrase; to me it sounded like a magical oath. His voice was cold and calculating, devoid of mirth. I'd never heard him speak like that before. My gut clenched, but I ignored it.

'Anything,' I agreed, still sobbing. 'Just save her.' My hands were stained red with Lucy's blood, and I couldn't look at the ruin I had wrought on her body. I rocked back and forth. I was on the floor. I didn't remember sitting or, more accurately, falling onto it.

Suddenly Wilf was in his wolf form, huge and beastly, black and white with streaks of gold. He was bigger than Archie had been, nearly as big as Gato. He stepped closer to Lucy and started to rend her flesh with his teeth. I closed my eyes and cried, but I couldn't close my ears. The sounds of him ripping, tearing and – God above –

eating. How could Lucy survive this? How could *anyone* survive this?

It seemed to last an age. I rocked back and forth, sobbed hysterically and waited for it to end. I covered my ears with my blood-soaked hands but still the noises of Wilf's feast penetrated my brain. I knew I would hear it in my nightmares.

Finally, the sounds stopped.

'She's healing,' Wilf said with satisfaction. 'She's going to make it.'

More tears poured down my cheeks as I realised that I hadn't killed my best friend. The stench of blood hung heavy in the air, but when I finally persuaded my eyes to open, Lucy had stopped bleeding. Dried blood painted her skin but none of it was fresh. Her skin, which had been wan and ashen for weeks, was already glowing with health. She murmured in her sleep and rolled over.

Wilf was back in human form, naked and covered in Lucy's blood. I looked away quickly. He laughed. 'So prudish, Jinx.' His tone was light and teasing. 'I've put on a housecoat,' he assured me. 'You can look at me now.'

I met his laughing eyes. 'Not all of us are casual about nudity,' I said, sticking my tongue out at him. I desperately needed to recover my equilibrium because I was one sharp move away from losing my shit completely. I needed banter to stabilise myself. I'd been careening from grief and fear for weeks, all the while with this last desperate option hiding in my heart. There had been no guarantee that Lucy would survive a transformation – and there was definitely no guarantee she'd be happy about being turned into a werewolf and forced into a realm she had no idea existed. *I* would choose it over death, but would she? It was moot anyway; she hadn't chosen it, I'd chosen it for her. And I hoped she would forgive me for playing God with her life.

'Will she be okay now?' I asked in a small voice.

Wilf slung an arm around my shoulders and kissed me on the forehead. 'Yes. She's a wolf now, even if she doesn't know it yet. She's healing – the ones that don't transform don't heal. You saved her life Jinx.' *True*. He grimaced. 'I'm going to have fun explaining this one to the council.' *True*. 'They're not going to be happy with me. We're supposed to petition the council for permission for an unsanctioned turn.'

I frowned. 'But wouldn't that make it sanctioned?'

'By the council, not by the Connection.'

'If the council aren't the Connection, then who are they?'

'The wolf council. Generally, each species still has its own ruling system, except for the ghouls.' He read my blank expression and continued. 'For the wolves we have the council. For the vampyrs there are the clans. The dragons have the Prime, and trolls have their Elders. Then of course, there's the Connection.'

'Our overlords and masters,' I quipped.

Wilf shrugged. 'Politics are not my forte.' He gave me another kiss on the forehead. 'You'd better go. We'll take care of Lucy. She's not going to come around for a while yet.'

'I should be here to explain to her about the Other,' I protested.

Wilf shook his head. 'She's a wolf now. She needs time to adjust and she needs to spend time with the pack. She doesn't need reminders of who she was, not until she's got her head around who she *is*.'

I frowned. 'She's the same.'

'No, she's a wolf. She'll never be the same as she was. But she will live, Jinx.' *True.*

I scrubbed my face with my hands. I hoped Lucy would forgive me. Maybe then I could forgive myself.

CHAPTER 4

I OPENED THE car door and slid into the back with Gato. When I turned to him, he hooked his massive head over my shoulder in a hug. I drew in a shuddering breath. 'I stabbed her,' I explained quietly to him and Nate. 'And then Wilf turned her. She's going to live. As a wolf.'

I met Nate's eyes in the rear-view mirror. He could feel the horror and self-doubt churning through me. 'You saved her,' he reassured me.

'Maybe. But I also condemned her to be a werewolf without talking to her about it. She's going to be pissed.'

'Better pissed than dead.' Nate started the car. 'Home?' he asked.

I hadn't been home in nearly four weeks. 'Lucy's,' I said finally. 'I need to shower and I need to sleep.'

Lucy hadn't given Nate permission to enter her home, so he couldn't come in. I needed some support right now but I was lousy at asking for it. Gato would do. I'd cried on him many a time. For now I needed my composure because I had another call to make.

'Hello?' Lucy's mum answered straight away.

'Hi, Sandy. It's Jinx.'

'Jinx, what the hell is going on?' Her voice was laced with anger and fear, and I felt responsible for both.

'I'm sorry, the Hoppas Centre called about a room just after you left. We contacted them as soon as we knew Lucy was sick but they didn't have a place on the programme. A slot opened, and Lucy had already signed the forms giving them permission to collect her if there was a vacancy. I've had a call. She's been having treatment on the plane, and they said she's responding well.'

'She's responding to it?' Sandy asked, her voice trembling. Her hopeful tone was painful.

'Yes. We'll know more soon. Go to bed, Sandy. I'll call when I hear from them again.'

Lucy's mum was exhausted, and it didn't occur to her to query why I was the Hoppas Centre's contact, nor what this miracle treatment was. She was probably too tired – and too hopeful.

We said our goodbyes and rang off. I was shattered and I fought to stay awake in the car. I dimly heard Nate on the phone. 'She needs you.' Then I was out for the count.

I OPENED MY eyes blearily as I was carried out of the car.

Emory was carrying me. He smelled entirely too good. 'Hey,' I managed.

His gaze sharpened before a soft smile lit his face. 'Hey, sleepyhead. Let's get you cleaned up.'

Nate opened Lucy's front door with the key and then went back to my car to settle in for the night. Sometimes being a vampyr sucked. Immortal life, super speed, healing spit … but shitty accommodation when you couldn't get permission to go inside a house.

Emory carried me in, cradling me all the way upstairs to the bedroom I used when I stayed at Lucy's. He started to unbutton my shirt.

'Hey!' I objected, stilling his hands. 'I can do this bit.' I was blushing. It felt like it was a lifetime ago that Emory and I had got hot and heavy in the back of a limousine. We'd talked loads over the last few weeks but mostly on the phone. Now was not going to be the first time he saw me undressed. Not when I was a hot mess. Or just a mess.

'I've seen you shirtless before,' he reminded me.

I gave him a flat stare. 'When?'

'After the vampyr's attack at Black Park.'

I narrowed my eyes. 'You turned around!'

He smirked. 'Windows have reflective surfaces.'

'Out!' I glared, pointing to the door. 'This is not how you are going to see me naked for the first time!'

'But I'm really good in the shower…' he promised.

I continued to point to the door.

'Fine,' he conceded. 'I'll go and sort us some food.'

As if on cue, my stomach rumbled. I couldn't even remember when I'd last eaten. I'd had a flapjack from the hospice vending machine for breakfast. The staff had offered tea and toast, but who can eat when their best friend is visibly dying in front of them?

Emory let out a sharp whistle and Gato came charging up the stairs. 'You're on duty,' he instructed. Gato gave an affirmative bark.

I rolled my eyes at both of them. 'I'm fine. And no one is after me at the moment, so we're good.'

'Let's try to keep it that way for at least a week,' Emory suggested.

'You just don't know how to have fun.'

His green eyes flashed. 'Oh, I know all about fun, and I'll teach you about it, as soon as you can string a sentence together.'

I stuck out my tongue and ignored him. He was right: I really was shattered. I didn't want him to see how much effort I was expending in pretending to be all right. I was as far from all right as I could be. God, what had I done to Lucy?

Emory left the bedroom and went down to the kitchen. I made my way into the Jack-and-Jill bathroom, peeled off my blood-soaked clothes and stepped into the hot shower. The water ran pink and it made me feel queasy on a lot of levels. Queasy. Guilty. Horrified. I started to cry again. The hot tears streamed down my face and mixed with the hot water.

Stubbornly pulling myself together, I showered slowly with lethargic movements and many stifled yawns. Finally I stepped out and dried off. I towelled my hair and shoved it back into a messy bun. No doubt I'd regret it tomorrow, but it was a quick and easy solution for now.

I borrowed one of Lucy's silk pyjama sets. It was soft pink and entirely too girly for me, but it made me feel close to her. I hoped she was okay. I hoped she wasn't scared. I bit my lip, feeling like a terrible friend. The guilt was crippling me.

Gato barked at me and nudged me towards the door. 'Food, huh? Are you hungry, too?' In answer, he pushed past me and thundered down the stairs ahead of me, making me laugh. 'Sorry, pup, let's get you sorted.'

I walked into the kitchen diner and stopped. The dining room table was laden with food and lit by candlelight. I blinked. 'How long was I showering?' I asked incredulously.

Emory had shucked off his business suit and was now in jeans and a T-shirt – black, of course. His chin was sporting a hint of growth, and now that I was looking properly, he looked a little weary. I checked the time: 10 p.m. 'Are you okay?' I asked him. 'You look tired.'

'All this gourmet cooking,' he joked.

'Did you cook *any* of it?' I asked, studying the table.

'No, but I did cut up the cheese.' He pointed at the cheese board laden with generous slices of brie, grapes and crackers. In the centre of the cheeseboard was a baked camembert and a French baguette. Next to it there was a pot of chilli and rice, crisps, biscuits and olives. It was a buffet for an army – but just for us two.

'I'm not going to eat all of this,' I protested.

'Don't worry,' he assured me. 'I'll make a fair dent in it.'

We sat down and conversation was temporarily suspended in favour of shovelling in food as fast as we could. The baked camembert had been studded with rosemary and garlic. It was also flavoured by my extreme hunger and may, in fact, have been the best thing I'd ever tasted. After a good half an hour of eating, I held my hands up in defeat. 'I'm done,' I admitted.

Emory grinned. 'You did pretty well for a human. You can put away food.' His tone was approving.

'Sometimes I eat salad,' I said defensively. I do, but only if it has halloumi or chicken. I'm not into rabbit food.

We moved to the living room to let the food settle before bed. Emory put on some music and we sat next to each other on the sofa, each with a glass of red wine.

I yawned and leaned on him. He stretched out his arm and settled it across my shoulder, bringing me closer. I snuggled in. The music was soft. It was going to take all my will power to stay awake. Luckily I had Emory to focus on and, man, was he worth focusing on.

We talked about music and movies and food and other inconsequential things, avoiding mention of politics and stabbing our best friends. When I finally relaxed into the conversation and got my courage up, I decided to apologise. 'I've been rather self-centred the last few weeks,' I confessed.

Emory's lips curved upwards. 'With good reason.'

'Sure, but still … I haven't really made time for you.'

'I'm not a pet,' he retorted, amused. 'You don't need to give me a fixed amount of attention.'

I pushed away from him. 'You're not making this easy,' I huffed. 'I'm trying to apologise for being a bad … whatever.'

He was grinning openly now. 'You're not a bad whatever, you're a good whatever. I've enjoyed whatevering with you.'

I glared a little harder. 'So I have commitment issues. Surely that doesn't come as a surprise? Besides, girlfriend and boyfriend just sounds ridiculous. We're dating, right?'

'Right,' he agreed, still smirking.

Best to change the subject. 'Anyway, thanks for being here.'

He leaned forwards and kissed me swiftly on the lips, just the barest brush of his lips on mine. 'No problem,

Jess.'

My tummy was churning, and for the first time in weeks it was in a good way. I was smiling, and I couldn't seem to stop. I felt lighter than I had in a long time. At least something in my life was going the right way.

'So how have things been with you the last few weeks?' I asked. 'Mostly we've been talking about me and Lucy.'

Emory frowned. 'They've been better,' he admitted. 'One of our younglings has been sick. It's very unusual for us to catch any kind of virus or bug, but she's been really ill and she hasn't regained consciousness. I've heard rumours that the trolls have been getting sick too, but our communication lines aren't exactly open.' He ran a hand through his hair. 'We've set up camp at the hospital so she can receive the best medical attention. We've also called in the healing wizards and witches, but though she's stable, she's not improving, and we don't know why.'

Then he made an effort to lighten the mood. 'And, of course, I've been haunting the archives and hounding the Elders for you. So it's been busy.' His tone was light but tiredness lined his face. He hadn't given up on finding a solution for me, and having one of his people so sick must have been a real worry. I guessed it was unusual for an immortal species to get sick.

I had the impression that dragons weren't a prolific

species, so young dragons were rare. They were cared for and spoilt. I tried to envision a young Emory growing up in the lap of luxury but it was hard to imagine him as a child. I preferred to imagine he'd sprung into the world fully formed and totally sexy.

'I'm sorry you've been going through all that and I haven't been supporting you. But thank you for all your help,' I said sincerely. It was my turn to kiss him. When I pulled away, his smile was like the sun coming up.

'You're welcome,' he murmured and pulled me back down for a longer, slower kiss that left my mind blank.

'I like you,' I blurted out.

His lips tipped up at the edges. 'I like you too.' *True.*

'Cool,' I said. 'Glad we had this chat.'

Emory's phone pinged and he pulled it out of his pocket, still keeping his arm around me. 'Sorry,' he murmured, 'I just need to check this. The only downside to being the Prime is always being on call.' He read the message, and I averted my gaze from the phone to give him some privacy. He noted the movement. 'I don't plan on having secrets from you. Relationships don't end well in those circumstances.'

'And you want it to end well?'

There was a moment of heavy silence. 'I don't want it to end at all.' *True.*

I grinned at that. Just because it was true now didn't mean it wouldn't be a lie in the future, but right now it was nice to hear. I didn't want this thing between us to end either. I still didn't know Emory through and through, but I was really interested in knowing him better. And not just in the carnal sense.

'Me too,' I agreed. We exchanged a warm glance before Emory gave his phone his attention again.

He frowned. 'You know Jack Fairglass?' he asked out of the blue.

'I know him. He fished me out of the sea one time after a sabotaged skydive.'

That diverted him momentarily. 'Did you find the saboteur?'

'Yup, and he's dead so there's no need to look so murderous.'

Emory's scowl eased. 'Good,' he said, sounding satisfied. 'You'll have noticed justice is somewhat different in the Other realm.'

'Rough and ready.' I thought about Stone's swift beheading of the vampyr who attacked us.

'You've got to prove you're strong, or you're judged weak. Now we're dating, if someone tries to harm you, that's a "fuck you" to both you and to me. It has to be answered or we'll be judged weak. If that happens, I could lose my position.'

I swallowed. That seemed all a bit mad and the feminist in me objected. The Other was something else. 'So if I get attacked, am I supposed to wait for you to rescue me like some sort of damsel? If I kill the attacker myself, will it look bad that you didn't kill them?'

'Oh no,' he assured me. 'It makes you strong, too. As long as one of us deals with it, or one of my men, it's fine. It just can't go unanswered.'

I blew out a breath and added it to the ever-growing rolodex of the weirdness of the Other. 'Anyway,' I asked, mostly to change the topic. I'd deal with this another day – any other day. 'What did Jack want?'

'One of the girls on shore leave has returned. She was delirious when she arrived back.'

'Shore leave?' I asked.

'Think rumspringa but for mermaids,' Emory explained. 'When they reach twenty-one, they get to have a year on land away from the shoal. They let their hair down, discover their legs and have a great time. After a year, they return to the shoal and settle into normal life. So this girl, she returns from shore leave and she's not talking sense. She had a fever and was delirious, and now she's passed out. Jack is very concerned. He thinks it's a virus and wants to know if any of the dragons have had anything similar. Our genetic material isn't so different and we're susceptible to similar illnesses – which is to say not many illnesses at all.'

'Does it sound similar to your dragon youngling's symptoms?'

He nodded slowly. 'Yeah, it sounds similar. And Jack

says the healing wizards and witches haven't been able to help the mermaid.'

'Is that unusual?'

'It's unusual for dragons to get sick, let alone for it not to be curable. Mermaids have a normal life span, but they're pretty robust. I don't like this. It was bad enough when it was just one of my people, but if it's the merpeople and the trolls too ... this could be really bad for us all.'

'Are any of the brethren sick?' I asked.

Emory shook his head. 'No, just the dragons so far.'

'Did they all eat similar foods, go to a Common place?'

He raised an eyebrow. 'No and no. You're thinking poisoning?'

'A bug that comes out of nowhere, that affects super-strong invincible dragons? Yeah ... I don't think this is the flu.'

He smiled. 'We're not invincible. We don't die of natural causes but we can be killed, or we can give up our immortal life span.'

I blinked. 'Why in heck would you do that?'

He tucked a stray curl behind my hair. 'There are advantages.'

'To giving up immortality? There'd better be!'

Emory's phone buzzed, and he read the message. He turned to me. 'Are you up for visiting the merfolk with me tomorrow?'

'Sure.' I yawned. 'Wilf has ordered me to leave Lucy alone for now so she can adjust, and I haven't exactly got a busy social calendar. But if I'm going to be helpful tomorrow, I'd better get some sleep.'

'You head on up. I'll ring Jack and discuss a few things, then I'll come up.'

'Okay. Good night, Emory.' I gave him a chaste kiss on the cheek.

I let Gato outside to do his business and left Emory to phone Jack. When Gato was done, we went upstairs. I brushed my teeth and fell into the double bed. In moments, I was asleep.

CHAPTER 5

I WOKE UP with a gasp. My heart was racing, and I was slick with sweat, and not in a sexy way. I scrubbed my eyes and desperately wished I could un-see the vision of Lucy covered in blood. I took some deep breaths and visualised the beach and the waves. Finally, my heartbeat slowed, and I started to feel calm again.

I sank back into the welcoming bed, but the sheets were cold and damp. I seriously considered ignoring that and going back to sleep, but unfortunately my bladder disagreed with my back-to-sleep plan. I sighed, peeled open my eyes and looked blearily towards the clock.

Obscuring the alarm clock was an arm. Not my arm. I had a moment of confusion and panic. I looked at my slumbering male companion. Emory. I racked my brains but couldn't remember him coming to bed, let alone anything happening. I needed to pee too much to worry about it. He must have been tired as well if my tossing and turning hadn't woken him.

I slid out of the bed carefully and nearly tripped over Gato, sprawled out on the bedroom floor. He lifted his head and gave me a baleful glare. He'd clearly been vamoosed from the bed and he wasn't thrilled about it. I patted the bed next to Emory. Gato heaved himself and lay down, content.

I went into the bathroom and dealt with the most pressing issue, then splashed some water on my face and left the bathroom through the other door into Lucy's room. I was awake now, so I'd better to do some self-care. I'd neglected myself the last few weeks and it was time to get things back on track.

I grabbed Lucy's jogging clothes and some trainers. It was the second week in January and it was bitterly cold outside. I got dressed quickly and headed down. In the kitchen, I had a glass of water and checked the time: 6:30 a.m. – no wonder it was still dark outside. Never mind, I was awake now and I needed a run to clear my head. I took the door key and headed out.

Nate was sleeping in my car. I knocked lightly on the door jamb, and he was alert instantly. He yawned and unlocked the car, then took in my clothes. 'We going for a run?' he asked.

'If you're up for it. Gato and Emory are still sleeping but I'd quite like the company.'

'Me too,' he agreed, climbing out of the car. He locked up and started to roll his neck.

'Sorry for the rubbish accommodation,' I apologised.

'My choice to stay. Besides, I've slept in worse.'

'Coffin?' He smirked and didn't answer. 'Ready?' I queried,

'I was born ready,' he replied, flashing me a grin.

We set off. He matched my pace easily, so I pushed a little harder. The cold was like breathing in shards of ice but my body soon warmed up and I stopped noticing. We ran on the roads and across the village green. The paths were flat and rather boring. I prefer running in woods or a park, but this was better than nothing. We ran for half an hour, and I guess we covered about six kilometres. Nate still hadn't broken a sweat. We cooled down by walking round the block.

'So that wasn't even a hard workout for you?' I asked.

Nate laughed. 'Vampyr.'

I rolled my eyes then a thought occurred to me. 'So what happens if someone in the Common hears you say vampyr? Will they just think you're nuts or that you're messing about?'

'The Other realm takes its protection seriously. Anyone in the Common will have heard me say "athlete", or something like that. The nearest applicable Common realm word will be shoved into their head. And if they saw me running as fast as I can really go, the Other would superimpose me on a motorbike or something similar. They're persuaded to see or hear the next rational explanation. Their minds do the rest.'

I let that sink in. 'That's pretty crazy. So you can't tell

anyone about the Other realm, even if you wanted to?'

'Exactly. The Other realm wants to stay hidden.'

'You talk about it like it's sentient.'

He sent me a lopsided grin. 'Who's to say it isn't?'

I stared at him incredulously. 'Food for thought, I guess.'

'What are your plans for today?' Nate asked.

'I don't know exactly, but at some point I'm going with Emory to meet Jack Fairglass.'

'The merman?'

I paused. 'I thought mermen and mermaids were secret.'

'From some, but not for us – vampyrs deal in secrets. But we respect their decision to stay out of the Connection. The wizards don't need to know everything, and they're not always clear-eyed when it comes to the creatures. I can see why the merpeople would bow out.'

'Do you consider yourself one of the creatures?' I asked curiously.

'No. For all we consume blood, we fall on the human side. Many of us aren't happy with how the Connection defines us. We've been spat on and called creatures over the centuries. We're not a popular race.' His tone was matter of fact.

'I guess being characterised as a creature isn't helpful?'

He shrugged. 'The word "creature" doesn't have the

same connotations as in the Common realm, and most of the creatures don't seem to take offence. Before the Verdict was agreed, there was a big movement to get us vampyrs killed or kicked out. Somehow the human side of things got a little more power and we landed on their side. We're neither creature nor human. The wolves are the same – half in, half out.'

'This place is nuts.'

'Maybe,' Nate said. 'But it's home.'

'Yeah, I hope so.'

He changed the subject. 'Fairglass is back up north. I imagine your Prime will have a helicopter or chauffeur-driven car sorted out for you. I'll drive your car to your home and park it there, then I'll check in with the clan. Just call me if you need anything.'

'Can you do some digging for me?' I asked. 'Some of the creatures have been getting sick – dragons, merpeople, maybe the trolls. Can you see if any vampyrs have been affected?'

'I'll try. But if Emory gets called away, give me a call.'

I frowned. 'I don't need a bodyguard.'

'How about a friend?' he offered. He threw me a wink, climbed into the car and drove off while I was still staring after him.

I felt myself smile. Yeah. A friend could work.

I let myself into Lucy's house and used the main bathroom to shower until I felt refreshed and vitalised. I got dressed in my usual jeans and T-shirt and headed downstairs. The smell of bacon was drifting on the air.

Emory looked up from his newspaper as I went into the kitchen. 'Hey, Jess. Did you sleep well?' He looked delectable as always in a sharp black suit and jet-black shirt.

'I did, thank you. Did you?' I didn't know how to address the fact that I'd woken up with him. His torso had been naked, and I'd thought about it a lot. I'd wondered if the rest of him was naked too. It had distracted me from my shower.

I flicked my eyes to the grill. It was closed, and a bit of grey was wafting out. Uh-oh. 'Generally, you leave the grill open,' I explained as I started across the kitchen. As I opened the grill door, a cloud of smoke billowed out. I grabbed the oven glove and pulled out the bacon. It was incinerated.

Emory got up from the table and came over. 'Not my finest work,' he commented airily.

I struggled to hold in a giggle. I loved the way he dealt with adversity. 'I like it crispy.'

Emory looked at the blackened strips. 'I think we're some way past crispy.'

'It'll be great with ketchup,' I said. *Lie.* My radar nearly made me lose my composure, and I coughed to hide a laugh.

As Emory opened the back door so the smoke could

escape, I fixed us bacon sandwiches spread liberally with butter and ketchup. Emory made us both a cuppa, and we sat at the table. He watched me, waiting for me to take the first bite.

I had to be brave; besides, I really did like crispy bacon. I took a bite. The taste of carbon filled my mouth. 'Mmm,' I managed.

Emory picked up our plates and tossed the food in the bin. 'Even Gato wouldn't eat that,' he muttered. He picked up his phone and hit speed dial. 'Breakfast,' he ordered and hung up.

'Has anyone ever told you that your phone manners suck?' I demanded.

He cast me an amused look. 'No.'

We nursed our brews and barely ten minutes later there was a knock on the door. Emory answered it and returned a moment later with a foil-covered tray of food. My tummy rumbled. 'Oh, thank goodness,' I murmured.

There were sausage sandwiches, bacon sandwiches, croissants and fruit, something for everyone. We wasted no time descending on the feast. 'Thank goodness we're both foodies,' I remarked.

'One of the finest pleasures in life,' Emory agreed.

'So where are we meeting Jack today?'

'On the Wirral. I've organised a helicopter.'

I grinned. 'Is that the only way you travel?'

'It's my favourite way. And if you've the money to

indulge yourself, why not?'

I couldn't really argue with that, though I didn't have the money to chuck away on helicopter rides. My business did all right but I'd been AWOL for a month, and the bills had a way of stacking up. I'd have to dip into my inheritance if I didn't get my ass into gear soon. Usually that was all the impetus I needed.

'What time do we need to leave?' I asked.

Emory checked his watch. 'In about forty-five minutes.'

'I'll go and pack.'

'I'll clear up here,' Emory offered.

I kissed his forehead and pushed myself away from the table, then went room to room grabbing all of my stuff. I'd been pretty much living here for a month while I was working the last case and Lucy was sick – and I wasn't a tidy house guest. My mum used to tease me that I was a messy girl because I was an only child. When I'd suggest she tidied up for me, she'd raise an eyebrow and say, 'What did your last slave die of?' to which I'd always reply, 'Underwork.' Witty, I know.

I felt a pang of sadness. I'd have given anything at that moment to have some banter with her again.

I dragged myself back to the present, finished packing and was ready to leave with five minutes to spare. I brushed on some mascara, lipstick and a bit of blusher. My skin was clear enough that I didn't really need foundation. I slung on my leather jacket and reached into the pocket, feeling relieved when I encountered nothing but fabric. No Glimmer lurking today. It was back wherever it went.

We locked up the house and Emory, Gato and I trooped off to the village green. I'd like to say that I wasn't just as thrilled as I was the first time I rode in a helicopter, but that'd be a lie. I felt a huge grin stretch across my face as it approached. It was the same pilot as last time.

'Do you *own* the helicopter and pilot?' I asked incredulously. I'd assumed that Emory had hired them.

'I own the helicopter. It's frowned on to say you own a person these days. The pilot is on a retainer.'

I stuck my tongue out at him. 'Smart ass,' I muttered.

Emory helped me into the back, and Gato leapt in happily. Even Emory was smiling; we were all happy to be flying. Before long we pitched up and were off. I glued my face to the windows the whole way. I love flying; I love seeing all the teeny-tiny houses and fields beneath me.

I looked at Emory. His legs were stretched out and he was lounging back, watching me indulgently. 'You're missing the view!' I pointed out.

He winked. 'I've got the best view in the whole place.'

I felt myself blush. I'm not good with compliments, and I didn't know what to say, so I went back to looking out of the window. Emory obviously enjoyed making me blush, and I heard him laugh quietly.

It took us just under an hour and a half to reach our destination, which was certainly better than chugging away in a car for four hours. Having said that, I'd definitely have enjoyed another go in Emory's Mercedes…

We set down on a beach. The tide was out. 'Where are we?' I asked.

'West Kirby. We've timed it perfectly – it's three hours from high tide.'

'And the tide matters because…?'

'We're meeting them on Hilbre Island.'

'Them?'

'Jack will be bringing the girl, and maybe some others.'

'How long does it take for us to get to this island?'

'It's about a two-mile walk across the sands.'

I looked dubiously at Emory's suit. My jeans and trainers were fine for a hike, but suits weren't the best attire.

'We could get the chopper to fly us there but I thought we'd enjoy the walk,' he suggested.

'That sounds nice. Does this count as our second date?'

He grinned. 'I think we're past second date stage, don't you?'

Third date stage usually involves some horizontal

44

mamba. 'Nope, definitely second date stage,' I teased.

We hopped out of the helicopter and Gato jumped down. He gave a big wag. He *loved* the beach. He looked at me. 'Go on,' I said, giving him permission.

His tongue lolled out in a doggy grin and he started running in a great burst of speed. He darted this way and that, tearing around the beach, leaving great impressions from his claws as he thundered about. 'He's having a mad moment,' I explained to Emory.

'He's having fun.' Emory flashed me a mischievous grin and then he bounded after Gato, running faster than should have been possible. Supernaturally fast. He ran around Gato; and Gato leapt up at him playfully. I laughed as they raced around each other like two lunatics. Eventually Emory returned to me. He still wasn't out of breath.

'Are you always that fast?' I asked curiously.

He winked. 'I promise I know how to go slowly too.'

I blushed and he laughed. He offered me his arm and we started walking out to the island together, all the while with Gato gambolling around us.

It was pretty much the best second date ever.

CHAPTER 6

W E WERE WALKING hand in hand on a beautiful sandy beach. If it had been warmer – and if we hadn't been due to meet some merpeople to talk about a sick girl – it would have been perfect. It was still pretty awesome. I take my highs where I can find them.

Emory took the lead as we approached the island, going first and checking the terrain was safe. I appreciated the thought. Normally I'm the type to hurtle into quicksand before realising there's a problem. He wasn't treating me like I was made of glass, but he was definitely being gentlemanly and it was nice. I know some feminists are anti being treated differently because of our gender, but I'm pro someone treating me kindly, male *or* female. I'd been looking after myself without respite for seven years, and the idea that someone might want to take care of me for once was hugely appealing. As long as Emory didn't expect me to do what he said, we'd be golden.

I could see a couple of structures on the island, but Emory didn't lead me towards them. Instead he took me to the other side where the tide was in. He led me down to the water's edge, and as we turned a corner, I saw a delegation of merpeople. Emory gestured for me to precede him.

Jack was already on the shore, his pale face was almost shining in the winter sunlight. His dark-green hair was tied back, giving easy access to his blue eyes. They shone like his scales once had, but it was easy to read the tiredness in them. Today Jack was scale-free; he had his land legs and was dressed in a power suit not dissimilar to Emory's.

In the water were four mermen and two mermaids. They were low in the sea with only their heads visible. I was pretty sure I recognised a couple of them from the trolls' stronghold. I gave them a finger wave, which they acknowledged with inclinations of their heads. No smiles today – everyone was on edge.

One of the merman's eyes looked gouged out but his head turned unerringly towards me. I swallowed a little. It felt creepy. There again, I'd been as quiet as an elephant when I climbed over the rocks. Even out in the sea he'd probably have heard me approach.

There was a young mermaid next to Jack. She was half in the sea and half laying on the rocks, her tail glittering in the sun. Her blonde hair stretched out on the grey stone, and she lay motionless. If I hadn't read the worry in Jack's eyes, I would have thought she was dead.

I'd met Jack a couple of times, and each time his

carefree attitude had been contagious. Today he was anything but free of care. 'Hey,' I greeted him. 'You're looking rough.'

Emory made a strangled noise next to me.

Jack flashed me a grin, a ghost of his former spirit. 'Jinx Wisewords. It's good to see you.' *True*. Well, that was nice.

'Good to see you, too. What's her name?' I gestured to the sprawled mermaid.

'Catriona,' he murmured. Everything in him softened. He loved her; the question was, as a sister or a lover?

Jack seemed to give himself an internal shake. He turned to Emory. 'Prime,' he greeted him and dropped to one knee. What the actual heck? I slid a 'what the hell' glance to Emory but he ignored it.

'Fairglass,' he said. 'Talk to me about Catriona. What do we know about her time frame?'

Jack stayed on one knee. 'We're reconstructing the last few days of her shore leave. We know for sure that she was in Liverpool. She had a flat, a job. The last time she was seen was two months ago. We've asked questions, but we haven't managed to meet her flatmate and gain entrance yet.' He frowned. 'This isn't in our skillset.' He looked pleadingly towards me. 'Can we hire you? I know you've been busy with your sick friend, but we need help. If I can retrace her steps and find out where she went missing, maybe we can work out what made her sick.'

Jack had helped me on a couple of occasions and I owed him. Besides, Mum always said it was important to help people. Be kind to one another. 'Sure,' I said easily. 'I'll need to take some details.' I pulled out my phone and switched on the notebook app.

Jack filled me in on Catriona's address and a few other details, including where she was working. She'd been a barmaid in town. When it was clear he was done, I glanced towards our silent audience in the water. 'Can we have some privacy?' I asked.

Jack dismissed his entourage with a jerk of his head, and they disappeared into the murky depths. I turned to Emory, exasperated. 'Can he get up now?'

Emory raised an elegant eyebrow but nodded. Jack stood up from the rock he'd been kneeling on. He didn't grouse or brush his knees like I would have done, he just looked at me expectantly.

I stepped over to Catriona and crouched next to her. I braced myself a little and reached out to touch her. Nothing. I frowned. I had touched a dead dragon and been transported into his dying moments, and I had felt Cathill's rage when I was in the same room as him. But from Catriona, there was nothing.

I turned to Jack. 'I'm sorry. I can't get a read off her.' Despair flicked across his face. 'It doesn't mean there's not something there,' I assured him hastily. 'I'm new at this empath stuff. It just happens or not.'

Jack made understanding noises but I could see he'd been hoping I'd get some sort of clue from her. 'Sorry,' I muttered again. It looked like we'd come all this way for nothing and it was my fault. Jack had asked Emory specifically for me, probably because he knew I was a truth seeker, but Catriona was keeping her secrets – or I didn't know how to read them.

Gato had been waiting patiently. Now, as he made his way carefully down to the mermaid, his claws clicked and scraped on the rocks. He sniffed her and let out a low whine then he turned to me, his eyes baleful.

'It's not natural,' I murmured. 'Whatever's wrong with her, it's not natural.'

Jack scrubbed a hand across his face. 'Unnatural is something.' There was relief in his tone. 'I can fight unnatural.'

Emory watched it all, his face impassive. 'Take her back to the shoal,' he instructed. 'We'll be in touch.'

That was it: Jack was dismissed. He didn't frown or bellyache but carefully cradled Catriona against his chest and walked into the sea, suit and all. Lover, then. He disappeared under the cold surface.

'Do his clothes just melt away?' I asked Emory curiously.

He looked amused. 'I've never asked. Come on, let's head back before the tide comes in again or we'll be stuck here for five hours.'

We started to walk back along the firm sands. 'So,' I started after a good ten minutes of awkward silence, 'you're what? King of the merpeople, too?'

Emory shrugged and didn't answer. I tugged my hand out of his. Stone had decided what information I needed and when, and he'd compelled me to trust him. Emory hadn't compelled me; I was getting there all by myself. But right now loud sirens were shrieking in my head. I wasn't going to be in a relationship with someone who couldn't be straight with me.

Emory reached out to take my hand again and I drew it back. 'I'm not interested in being made a fool of,' I said tightly. 'I can't have everyone else around you knowing who or what you are, and I'm there like a simpleton knowing nothing.'

'I've taken oaths,' Emory said finally. 'You're a wizard, you're human. It complicates things.' *True.*

'You can't tell me what's going on?'

'No. I'm sorry. But you're smart, you'll work it out.'

I didn't like that there was a puzzle I didn't even know the shape of.

'I can explain a few generalities,' Emory went on. 'You've noticed that there are ... tensions in the Other realm. Some species don't get on with others. Some think that not all of the species were created equal.'

I had a hundred questions but not many I thought he

might answer, so instead I asked, 'You guys think you were created?'

His lips curved upwards. 'That's your take away?'

'You have a big bad secret you can't tell me about. I'm a PI. I'll dig. But in the meantime … does the Other have a religion I don't know about?'

He shook his head. 'No. It's the same as the Common. A bit disappointing, I guess.'

'Not really,' I disagreed. 'Everything in the Other is weird. If you had a religion, you'd probably be doing human sacrifices.'

'You have such an upbeat perspective.' His voice was heavy with sarcasm. *Lie.*

Thanks, radar, I caught that one. 'I love that you have to always tell the truth except for when you're being sarcastic. I bet dragons are super-sarcastic all the time.'

'We have our moments,' Emory agreed. He touched my hand, and this time I let him. 'So,' he said, 'you told Fairglass you're a truth seeker?' It wasn't really a question.

'Yeah, a little bit.'

Emory slid me a sidelong glance. 'Is there anyone you haven't told?' he asked drily.

'I swore him to secrecy!' I protested. I paused. 'And the room full of trolls and mermaids. And the dryad.'

Emory groaned and did a face palm. 'Great.'

'What?' I objected. 'The troll Elder bound them to

secrecy.'

He exhaled loudly. 'Well, that's something. Can you try to not tell anyone else?'

'I don't see what difference it makes. I'm not exactly an asset right now, am I? I couldn't even get a read off that poor girl. Nothing. Nada.'

Emory tugged my hand, and we stopped walking. 'You're always an asset. It's not your fault that it didn't work. You haven't been taught anything, and you're learning as you go. I know how that feels and it's not great. You remember I said I knew one other empath?'

I nodded, my heart rate speeding up. To meet another empath would be amazing. I'd been adrift for so long that some direction would be invaluable.

'She said she'd meet with you and teach you a little about it, if you like.'

It would be so good not to be fumbling along in the dark. Perhaps the empath could shed a little light on the shape of my Emory puzzle, too. 'Yeah,' I said as casually as I could, like it wasn't a huge deal to me. 'That'd be fine.'

Emory grinned. I wasn't fooling him even a little bit.

We started walking again. Gato wasn't frolicking now; his experience with Catriona had sobered him. Instead he padded alongside us, his great head moving to and fro. I realised he was looking for threats.

A chauffeur-driven Maybach awaited us at the marina, and we climbed in. The car gave luxury a new meaning: even Gato fitted in easily. Emory rattled off my home address to the driver then engaged the privacy screen. He pulled me onto his lap. 'You're still upset with me,' he said softly.

'With the situation,' I countered.

His eyes scanned mine. 'I'd tell you if I could.' *True.*

'I know.'

He leaned forwards, giving me plenty of time to pull away. I didn't. I let his lips touch mine, and I let my mind switch off. Sometimes it was so good just to *feel*. He made me feel safe and wanted, and both were rare for me.

I shifted against him and felt his enjoyment of our current situation. It made me moan into his mouth. He pulled back, his eyes dark and full of promise. 'We're here,' he said.

'Huh? What?'

Emory gave a self-satisfied smirk. 'We're at your house, Jess.'

I blinked several times. 'How long were we kissing for?'

'Not long enough.' He gave me a fast peck. 'I've got a few things to attend to. I'll speak with the empath and talk to you later.'

I unstraddled his lap awkwardly, feeling like I'd been doused in cold water. 'Right you are then,' I said. I opened the door for me and Gato before Emory could.

'Catch you later.'

I marched up to my front door and opened it without looking back. After I closed it behind me, I slid to the floor and covered my face with my arms. 'Right you are then?' I groaned aloud. I was such a geek.

CHAPTER 7

I MADE MYSELF a late lunch and decided it was time to face up to a few calls I'd been avoiding. The first was to Wilf. He assured me that Lucy was doing well. She'd come round that morning and was being supported in learning how to change.

I tried to dig a little more, but Wilf told me bluntly it was wolf business; Lucy had her own phone, and she'd call me when she was ready. I passed on my lie about Lucy going to the Hoppas Centre and asked him to tell Lucy that I was going to inform her family that she was getting on well there. In a week or two she could have a miraculous remission and recovery.

Next I rang Lucy's mum, Sandy. I felt awful about the ongoing deception but there wasn't much else I could do. I told her that Lucy had arrived safely at the centre and was responding extremely well to the treatment. I told her the staff were cautiously optimistic. She cried and I felt awful all over again.

When my parents died, Sandy had often extended invitations to me. I'd refused them more often than not because I was hurting, and a wounded animal often lashes out. She'd never held it against me and had continued to support me despite the way I'd behaved. Even though I had deliberately created the distance between us, I still cared about her. After all, she had raised the most wonderful human being I knew.

I logged onto my laptop and my work emails. Hes had kept on top of everything but there were a still a few matters that needed my attention. There was a new request for a background check from a current client, so I spent the next hour exploring various identity checkers as well as trawling through the potential new hire's social media platforms. I typed up a dossier of information and an invoice. It felt good to do something normal.

I sent out a general email to my client mailing list, thanking them for bearing with me during a difficult time but assuring them I was now open for business as usual. Almost immediately I got a ping back asking if I could serve some papers that afternoon. I answered in the affirmative and ran off to the lawyer's office in Bebington. I picked up the divorce papers and served them in person in Birkenhead. Luckily the divorcee was home, so there was no need to make an appointment to come back or faff around with an affidavit of service. To cover myself, I took a picture of the recipient with the documents. I sent the lawyers the evidence of service and my invoice for same-day process service.

Evening was bearing down on me, but I felt like I'd accomplished a fair few things. It still bothered me that I hadn't been able to help Jack and Catriona. I picked up one of the books that Emory had sent me while I'd been looking for a miracle for Lucy and flipped through it, hoping to read something about empaths. Nada. I scanned the contents' pages of all the books until a heading about dragons caught my eye. I flipped to the chapter.

I didn't know how accurate the information was, but it gave me pause. Apparently a dragon only ever had one true mate. Given that they were immortal, that seemed like a pretty raw deal, particularly when the book was at pains to point out that dragons had to mate with a human. Of course, two dragons could get it on but that union could never produce a child. The chapter detailed a little about the courting of a dragon's mate. Apparently food was an important component because taking care of your prospective mate was paramount. I tried hard not to think about what this meant about Emory and me. Were we doomed to fail? Was I only going to be a notch on his bed post? Frankly, that wasn't how I rolled. But I would age and die and Emory would stay young and beautiful, so how could we be anything other than a casual roll in the hay?

I put down the book. I was reading too much into this. So what if I wasn't Emory's one and only mate? I was twenty-five – I had plenty of time to find the one I was going to settle down with. For now I would relax and enjoy Emory's company. He was fun and kind, and he seemed to get me. Plus, I got to ride in helicopters. What was not to like?

Gato and I had dinner and went for an evening stroll around the block. I rang Hes and had a catch-up. I told her that Lucy had become a werewolf but I didn't say that I'd had to stab her myself. Hes and I were friends, but it was a new and fragile friendship. I didn't think we were quite in the place where I could tell her that I'd stabbed my best friend and listened to her being eaten by a wolf. Just thinking about it made me nauseous.

I went to bed early with Gato next to me. My head was whirling so I did some breathing exercises and meditation. Even so, it was a long time before sleep claimed me.

I WOKE TO the feeling of a wet snout on my forehead and the sound of Gato's low, threatening growl. My eyes snapped open, and I stared into his eyes. He'd portalled me into the Other.

'What the hell?' I said eloquently, my mind still tangled with my dreams. 'What?' My heart was hammering. 'Shush.' He cut off mid-growl but hopped off the bed. I followed him and blinked when I saw Emory half-hidden in the shadows in the corner of my bedroom, looking as surprised as I felt. Gato approached and sniffed him. Finally satisfied it was Emory and not some threat, my boy took himself off to use the bathroom.

'I let myself in,' Emory explained. He frowned. 'We need to get your house runed. I'll get someone to see to it today.' He pulled out his phone and typed out some instructions.

'What?' I repeated.

'Not a morning person, huh?'

'I am if I wake up right. For future reference, growling hell hounds are not right.' I sat up and scrubbed my eyes. 'How did you get in?'

'Honestly? I'm not entirely sure. I was outside, thinking about how I wished I was in your room and then … here I am.'

I drew back my curtains and looked out. It was still dark; the streetlamps were lit, casting long shadows. A thought tugged at me. 'Were you in the shadows?'

Emory considered. 'I was there,' he said, pointing to the wall of my room. Yup, he was in shade. 'Try walking into this shadow and walking out there,' I said, pointing to his entry point outside.

He gave me a long look but did as I suggested. He walked into the shadows, his expression saying he was expecting to bump into the wall, but a moment later he was in the shadows outside my house. He'd phased.

He looked up at me, his expression unreadable, then turned into the shadows again. He strolled out of nothing and into my room. 'You know what's going on,' he said evenly, sounding curious.

'Maybe. Yesterday when you ran really fast, was that unusual for you?'

He tilted his head, considering it. 'I've been a little faster than usual this last month or so,' he admitted. 'Why?'

'Do you remember when we got ambushed in Black Park by those vampyrs? I killed a couple of them with Glimmer.'

'Yeah, I remember,' Emory said slowly, not sure what I was driving at.

'You looked at Glimmer and held it. It cut you. And now you can phase into shadows and run fast. Just like a vampyr.'

He raised his eyebrows. 'You think Glimmer gave me a vampyr's skills?'

'Unless you know of another reason why you could suddenly start phasing.'

He shook his head.

I reached under my pillow and drew out my knife. Emory grinned. 'You sleep with a knife under your pillow?'

'Don't you?' I muttered. 'One last test.' I used the

knife to slice lightly into my pinkie finger. Nothing a plaster wouldn't fix if Emory couldn't heal it. 'Vampyrs have healing spit,' I said to him. 'Spit into the cut.'

'That seems rather unsanitary,' he murmured. Nonetheless, he moved closer to me and took my little finger in his hand. He drew it slowly into his mouth and swirled his tongue over it. I was braced for a sting of hurt but it never arrived. All I could feel was the warmth of his mouth.

His eyes were dark as he sucked on my finger. I definitely should not have had an answering pull that shot down right between my legs. Slowly he pulled my finger back out of his mouth and we both looked down at it. Nothing. Not a single mark. The cut was completely gone.

'Any cravings for blood?' I asked. 'Changes in diet?'

'Zero cravings for blood. Interesting.' His voice was calm.

He could keep his calm; I was freaking out. 'Oh shit. I've made my boyfriend into a vampyr! A dragon vampyr! Holy hell!'

He snorted. 'I'm not a vampyr, I just seem to have a few of their tricks. My heart is still beating, no craving for blood. This isn't on you, Jess, it was Glimmer.' He tilted his head to one side considering. 'Know thy enemy and know yourself, and in a hundred battles you will never be defeated.'

I blinked. 'Sun Tzu?'

He grinned. 'Yeah. You've given me a huge advantage over the vampyrs. I didn't know they could phase, could heal. This is going to be a game changer.'

I winced. I was giving away Nate's secrets and it didn't feel good, but none of this had been intentional. I hadn't meant to use Glimmer on Emory, not like I'd done with Lucy. My eyes widened. 'Oh man. Lucy! I used Glimmer on Lucy after I killed Ronan.' I swallowed hard. 'Lucy … she's going to have the ability to pipe.'

Emory let out a low whistle. 'The ability to pipe in a pack of werewolves…'

'Oh shit. I have to call her.' I really didn't want to, I wanted to hide from this call a little longer. I'd stabbed her and forced her into living in a magical realm. If she stopped talking to me, it would hurt like a bitch. I didn't know if I could come back from it – but I still couldn't bring myself to regret my actions. If I hadn't stabbed her, she'd be dead. Alive-and-Angry-Lucy was better than Dead-Lucy. But that didn't mean I was looking forward to the call.

Emory gave me a swift reassuring kiss then took himself off to search out some breakfast and give me some privacy. I checked the time. It was 7:15 a.m., still pretty early to deliver this kind of news, but now I'd made my mind up it was go time. I took a deep breath and dialled.

The phone rang twice and it took everything in me not to hang up. I wasn't a coward, so I held on. Lucy answered on the fourth ring. 'Hi, Jess,' she answered.

I tried to analyse her voice. It seemed pretty even, though she didn't sound her usual excited self. It was pretty hard to tell with just two syllables. 'Hey,' I replied. 'Luce…' I didn't know what to say. My voice trailed off into silence. 'I'm really sorry,' I said finally.

'For stabbing me, or for keeping an entire magical realm from me?' she asked.

I bit my lip. 'Um, both?'

The line went quiet. Finally, she spoke. 'I'm not mad at you for stabbing me. You saved my life. So thanks.' There was a but.

'You're welcome?'

She huffed a little. 'Yeah. But I'm mad you kept a whole realm from me. From *me*! I'm not just anyone. You couldn't tell me you can do magic? Like you're freaking Harry Potter and you never so much as alohamorared near me!'

'I've only known about it for a short while,' I explained hastily. 'Since I met Stone and searched for Hester. You remember that case?'

She made a noise. 'Lord Samuel didn't mention that,' she said finally. 'You promise?'

'Like not even three months. I still don't know what I am, and half the time I totally forget I can do magic. I'm the worst wizard ever.'

'Okay – that makes me feel better,' Lucy said, and I could hear the smile in her voice. 'You just got the jump on me. I can totally catch up.' There was her competitive edge that I knew and loved.

'You'll be running circles around me in no time,' I assured her.

'I will.' She spoke smugly. 'I'm insanely fast in my wolf form.'

'How is it?' I asked carefully.

She let out a little laugh. 'Jess ... when you change, I swear it's like a mini-orgasm. Once I got the change nailed, I spent most of yesterday swapping back and forth.'

I gave a snort of laughter. 'You won't need your rabbit vibrator now.'

'Nope,' she replied cheerfully. 'Just my wolf.'

I cleared my throat. 'Listen...'

She groaned. 'There's more? Why is there always more?'

'I don't know, I might be making a mountain out of a molehill. You remember Emory?'

'Smoking hot sexy guy? Yeah, I remember him.'

'Right, well he's a dragon and—'

'He's a freaking what?'

'A dragon. Yeah. When he's in his dragon form he's twenty feet long. Red scales, green eyes, gold wings. Full dragon. Everything you've ever imagined.'

Lucy let out a whistle. 'I love this bloody realm.'

Relief was pouring through me. Lucy was going to be okay. She wasn't mad, she was excited about the new realm. 'So anyway, it turns out he's got some vampyr traits—'

'Vampyr?!'

I paused. 'What has Wilf told you?'

She laughed. 'I'm sorry. I'm just messing with you on that one. He did actually tell me about vampyrs. Apparently, wolves and vampyrs are a no-no.'

'So are dragons and vampyrs. Sworn enemies, think Israelis and Palestinians. Centuries of fighting and bad blood between them. Anyway, long story short, Emory has some vampyr skills because I stabbed him with a magic dagger. It's the same magic dagger I stabbed you with too. And now you may have some extra piping skills.'

There was a pause while she tried to work it out. 'Like the ability to do some excellent cake frosting?'

'No, not that kind of piping. Think Pied Piper.'

'I can get rats to follow me?'

'Not just rats. Pipers can talk to, and manipulate, animals. Magical or otherwise. So the reason I thought I'd better tell you... Pipers can control werewolves when they're in their wolf form. It makes them unpopular with the werewolves.'

There was a long silence. 'I don't know what to do with this,' Lucy said finally.

'Honestly? I have no idea. But you probably want to keep it under your hat, and just be careful how you speak to wolves in their wolf form. Maybe get in some ants or something, and try on them first. Start small. I may be wrong, maybe you haven't got any extra skills, but Emory does and it stands to reason that you will, too. So watch yourself. It's why I rang.'

'Otherwise you would have avoided this call for weeks until I broke and called you first,' Lucy sassed.

'One hundred percent,' I confirmed, grinning. Then my grin faded. 'Lucy … I called your mum and told her you're doing okay at the Hoppas Centre, but maybe tomorrow you could call her? She doesn't deserve to worry. And she deserves a miracle, too.'

'I'll call,' Lucy promised.

'Remember to try to sound sick. You were dying.' My voice cracked and a sob slipped out. Suddenly I was crying in earnest. 'I couldn't help you,' I managed to say. 'You were dying.'

'You did help,' she answered, her own voice thick with tears. 'You saved me, honey.'

I gave a nod she couldn't see but it still took a good five minutes before the tears dried up. 'Sorry,' I said eventually. 'I guess it's all finally hit me.'

'Yeah, I get that. I wish I could give you a hug.'

'I wish you could, too. Any idea when you can go out and about?'

'Lord Samuel says I have to learn the ways of the wolf first. A week or two maybe.'

'Okay. I'd better go. You be careful.'

'All right.' She paused. 'My wolf says hi.'

'Your wolf? She's a separate being?'

'Yeah – Esme. You'll really like her. She's super kick-ass.'

I snorted. 'Your wolf is called Esme? Not "Deadly Fang" or something that *sounds* kick-ass?'

'Esme is very kick-ass, she doesn't need to prove it.' There was something like pride in Lucy's voice, and I was glad. She seemed to be adjusting to this werewolf business, and if she had a bad-ass companion riding shotgun I was pleased for her.

'So you can talk to your wolf?'

'Yeah. She's tough, no nonsense. You two would get on.'

'Is it normal to be able to talk to your wolf? Or do you think you can do it because you can pipe?'

'Oh hell, I have no idea. No one else has mentioned talking to their wolf. I thought it was just because it was a private thing…'

I winced. 'Luce, do some careful digging, but you'd better keep this to yourself. If you can talk – really talk – to your wolf, it gives you a huge advantage over the others. Archie said he kind of has to wrestle control, and he didn't make it seem like a happy partnership. Or a partnership at all, to be honest. If you and Esme can co-exist in harmony...'

'Yeah,' Lucy agreed. 'Heck, I'm not even going to be normal in the magical realm.'

'Normal is overrated. You're special. You've always been special to me.'

'Aww. You're so cute.'

I rolled my eyes. 'Take it back,' I said firmly. 'I am not *cute*. I am a bad-ass PI.'

She laughed. 'Yeah you're a real tough broad.'

'I am,' I insisted. My radar pinged. I'm not. 'I'd better go for real this time. You and Esme keep safe. Watch each other's backs, okay?'

'Esme says she's got this. Love you, Jess.'

'Love you so much, Lucy.' We rang off. I felt like a weight had been lifted off my chest. She forgave me; maybe now I wouldn't see her blood in my dreams.

CHAPTER 8

E MORY WAS WORKING his way through an entire box of cereal. He had the milk out and he just kept making up fresh bowls of Crunchy Nut. 'I'm going to have to fill up my larder if you're going to be a regular house guest,' I commented.

He flashed me a grin. 'Don't worry, I normally bring my own supplies. Today I planned to get breakfast before I disturbed you, but the phasing thing threw me.'

'Sure. It was surprising. So, what's your plan for to-day?'

'I thought we could get you some lessons in empathy.'

'What about Catriona?'

'I can get the brethren to dig into her job and her apartment while we work on your empathy. You need to learn how to use it, or your gifts will be hamstrung. There's never going to be a good day to get started.'

'I'll get Hes on it too,' I suggested. 'She can work with your brethren.'

Emory agreed readily. 'I'll get my second to contact Hes. Give me her number.'

I rattled it off, and he sent a text. His second was Tom Smith, and I wondered if that surname was real. I texted Hes his details and some information about the case. She replied quickly that today was a study day so she was free then sent me some big smiley-face emojis. She was excited to be on a case.

Hes had been stabbed by Glimmer after it had been used on Nate. I'd bet good money she now had vampyr skills though she hadn't mentioned anything to me. I made a mental note to talk to her about it later, though I wasn't quite sure how to start that conversation. 'So … does your spit do anything special?' Yup. Nailed it.

Gato and I ate breakfast and prepared for the day. I forewent my usual run in favour on getting the drop on learning about empathy. I was eager to get a handle on this shit because it was frustrating when it came and went whenever it felt like it. It was nothing I did consciously; one moment I could feel Cathill's rage, or a dead dragon's dying moments, and the next I got exactly zilch from Catriona. It was frustrating.

'How are we getting to your empath?' I asked.

'We'll drive.'

'What, no helicopter ride today?' I teased.

'No. No one knows her location, and I'm not letting anyone else in on that information.'

I blinked. 'You don't trust your helicopter pilot?'

'I do, but her safety is paramount. I won't put her at

risk.'

'You want me to be blindfolded?' I offered, only half-joking.

His lips twitched. 'In the bedroom? Sure. In the car? No, there's no need. Besides, you have to drive. I think it'd be frowned on if I blindfolded you.'

I blushed fuchsia. 'Right, yes, of course,' I managed to say. Of course I was going to drive; he didn't know how to. 'Can Gato come?' I asked.

'Of course.' Emory nodded at Gato, who gave a happy wag to be included.

We piled into my small Ford Focus. 'Remind me to get you a new car,' Emory commented.

'I love my little car. It's fine.'

'Keep the little car for surveillance, but you could do with a bigger one for longer journeys. You liked the Mercedes. You can have that.'

I rolled my eyes. 'Don't be ridiculous. We've been on like three dates. You are not giving me a 150,000 pound car.'

He ignored me, slid out his smartphone and tapped out a message. There was a whoosh when the email was sent.

'Did you just tell someone to transfer the Mercedes into my name?' I asked incredulously.

There was a pause. 'I don't think you'll like the answer to that question, so let's move on. Turn right here.'

I turned right. 'You don't need to buy my – affection. I already like you. I have my own money and I don't need yours. I could buy myself a Mercedes if I wanted.' I could. It might burn through literally *all* of my savings, but I could if I really wanted to.

Emory reached over and squeezed my thigh. 'I could buy you a car every single day for a year and still not make a dent in my wealth. Don't read too much into it. It's just a car.'

His hand on my thigh was distracting me so I lifted it off my leg and returned it to his lap. 'If you distract me, we'll crash,' I pointed out.

He returned his hand to my thigh and started gently running it up and down my leg. 'Is this distracting?'

I glared and pushed his hand back again. 'Quit it.'

He grinned but settled back, and this time he kept his hands to himself. I had to admit that I was a little disappointed.

He directed me while we drove for over an hour out of the Wirral and into the rural area surrounding Liverpool. Eventually he led us to a small lake; I had no idea there was a body of water this big so close to the city. We parked and he led the way into the woods. I felt for a moment as if I were lost in a Hansel and Gretel fairy tale. I was feeling upbeat about today so fingers crossed there were no cannibal witches about.

Emory took us to a clearing. The house that was in it

was as far from a cottage as you could get. It was a modern building, all glass and wooden cladding. The reflections of the trees bounced back off the windows, making it feel like it was somehow part of the woods.

The glass afforded its occupiers little privacy and I could see its two elderly occupants were at the breakfast table. Emory waved and the gesture was returned before the man came and opened the front door to let us in. There was something familiar about him.

'Prime, my boy!' he greeted Emory warmly. 'How good to see you. Come on in.' They hugged, the affection between them obvious.

The old man must have been ninety if he was a day. He moved with slow, shuffling movements and his back was hunched, like gravity was pressing down on him. He still had a full head of hair but it was all white. His face was lined and worn but his eyes were bright and clear. He smiled at me warmly in greeting. 'Jessica. Be welcome in our home. My name is Cuthbert.'

He stepped back from the door and held it open so we could enter. I had a nagging feeling that I'd seen him somewhere before, but I couldn't place it.

Emory went in first, kicked off his shoes and placed them by the door. 'Wipe your paws,' I muttered to Gato under my breath.

'No need to fuss,' the old man said. 'It's no problem if you track in a little mud.' He might have been old as the hills, but there was nothing wrong with his hearing.

I went to kick off my shoes. 'Don't bother,' Cuthbert said bluntly. 'You'll be needing them again soon enough.'

That stung a little. What a way to make me feel welcome. I guess he wasn't planning on me sticking around. I left on my trainers.

We walked out of the porch into a wall of heat. The house was boiling. Emory let out a sound of contentment and tugged off his suit jacket, then knelt at the old lady's feet. 'Prime,' he greeted her.

'No longer, my boy,' she chided gently. She kissed him. 'Prime *Elite*,' she greeted him, laying emphasis on the second half of his title.

Emory grimaced. 'Audrey,' he said, sounding dismayed. 'Not you, too. Emory, please.'

She ran her hands through his hair. 'Dear boy.' The affection in her voice was unmistakeable and I felt suddenly like I was intruding.

'Tea?' the old man asked me softly.

'Sure.' I decided to join Cuthbert in the kitchen, giving Emory a moment alone with Audrey. Gato looked between Cuthbert's retreating back and the two dragons, but finally decided to remain with Emory and sat at his feet.

Cuthbert didn't turn round from the tap. 'As I said, I'm Cuthbert. My lady is Audrey. My honour to meet you, Jessica.' He switched on the kettle and turned back to me, touching his hand to his heart and bowing.

I returned the gesture. 'My honour to meet you, Cuthbert. Thank you for welcoming me into your home. It's lovely and warm.'

'Dragons are reptilian, and they can only get warmth from their surroundings. Though they can cope well enough in the cold, they crave warmth. After being Audrey's mate for several centuries, I have to admit I've also become accustomed to the warmth.'

My mouth dropped open. 'Centuries? You're a dragon as well?'

'No,' he said easily, 'just a human. A wizard actually, though I use the IR less and less these days. I like modern conveniences.' He gestured to the kettle. It flipped off the boil and he poured the hot water into a large teapot.

'I don't get it,' I admitted. 'You're human and you've lived multiple centuries?'

'Five, I think. Give or take.'

I stared. Give or take what? Fifty years? A hundred? 'And that's possible how?'

'Well now, I'm giving away secrets.' He winked and continued. 'If you're a dragon's true mate, you can share in the dragon's lifespan. You get to have increased life and they accept decreased life. I'm telling you this because it seems to me that young Emory has his eye on you, so it's something you may want to know.'

I blushed. 'We're just dating.'

He smiled. 'That's how these things generally start. We don't tend to leap right in with the mating.' He winked again. 'When dragons find their true mate, it's a big deal. Emory will protect you with everything he has until you accept him.'

'I don't understand. He's not ... we're not...'

Cuthbert patted my hand. 'He's giving you time.'

The way he was talking made it seem like Emory and I were destined, and I didn't like that. My destiny was my own. I didn't believe in one mate, one true love. I believed there were lots of people out there who would fit me well enough. I hadn't found one yet, but they were out there. Stone, for example, might have fit me well enough.

Emory was ... well, he was hot and I really liked him a whole lot, but we still didn't know everything about each other. Surely mates should know each other inside out? Our fledgling relationship was going well but it wasn't enough for me to accept anything so dramatic as him being the other half of me. I shifted uncomfortably. Destined mates? No thank you.

Cuthbert looked at me like he knew what I was thinking. Maybe he did; maybe he'd thought it, too. He took a huge tin of biscuits out of the cupboard. 'Best to keep our dragons well fed,' he murmured, then placed it on a tray along with the pot of tea and some mugs.

'We've given them enough time alone, I reckon.' He gestured to the tray. 'Be a dear and carry it in for me. I've really slowed down this last century.'

'Of course.' I picked up the tray and followed his slow progress into the lounge. It was a huge open-plan space, and in it were two dragons stretched out along the length of the room, their necks intertwined in a regal hug. Emory was in all his red-and-gold glory; Audrey was red and gold too, but her scales were pale, leached of colour like a Monet impression of Emory. I could see her age in every slow and laborious movement.

Something tickled again in my brain. She felt familiar like Cuthbert. I worried at the thought, but the more I reached for it the more the knowledge slid away. I sighed. It would come to me eventually.

Cuthbert smiled softly at Audrey, his adoration clearly evident in his eyes. 'Stretching out, my love?' he called.

There was a shimmer and suddenly Audrey and Emory were back in their human forms. Audrey's hair was long and flowing, as white as Cuthbert's. Her face was lined and ravaged with age, but there was a warmth about her that appealed to me instantly. She looked like the quintessential grandma. 'Jessica Sharp,' she greeted me. 'It's good to see you.'

I could almost hear the unspoken 'again'. I blinked. 'Have we met before?'

Audrey smiled. 'Not yet.' Her smile widened. 'I can feel your confusion from here, child. Come closer.'

I wanted to object to the term child, but I guess when

you'd lived several centuries my twenty-five years might seem a little infantile.

I set the tray down on the table, and Cuthbert busied himself with pouring each of us a cup of tea. I liked that it was in mugs rather than teacups and fine china. No airs and graces here, for all Audrey had been the former Prime.

She patted the seat next to her insistently so I sat beside her. Emory was on the sofa opposite, legs stretched out, arms resting on the back of it. He would have looked casual if his eyes hadn't been following my every move. He was tense. I didn't know why but it was making me nervous.

Cuthbert passed me a mug doctored with milk and I nodded my thanks.

'No,' said Audrey decisively. 'This won't work. Emory, Cuthbert, off with you both.' She clapped her hands and made a shooing motion.

I expected some sort of objection from Emory but he stood and left the room instantly with Cuthbert following behind. Cuthbert shut the door carefully and I was left alone with Gato and an ancient dragon.

'He's a little too distracting for you, isn't he?' Audrey commented, sipping her tea. 'I remember those days well – should I mate with him or shouldn't I? All that tension. It's making you uncomfortable.'

I really didn't want to talk about *tension* with

Emory's ... whatever she was. 'I'm not sure I believe in all of this mate business,' I admitted instead.

'You're just as well not believing in the sun and the stars. Believe in it or not, it exists. Cuthbert and I are evidence of that. But you don't have to accept Emory, there are others that will suit you well enough. Your destiny isn't written in stone. Yes, you're *Emory*'s true mate, but humans have many true mates and you still have free will.'

I didn't know what to say. I was treading carefully here. Emory clearly had a great deal of affection and admiration for Audrey, so I wasn't going to insult her. She could be family, his mother, even. 'Are you related to Emory?' I asked, partly to change the subject and partly out of curiosity.

'No. I first met him in Liverpool when he was a street urchin. His mother had died in labour, his father was a drunk and a wastrel. His formative years were rough and lonely – and he didn't even know he was a dragon. He hadn't been properly introduced because he had no one. Poor lad. I'm eternally grateful he was brought to me. And I'm eternally grateful to the one who brought him to me. Cuth and I never had children. Emory was our gift.'

It made my heart hurt to think of a young Emory being hungry and alone. I'd been raised with nothing but warmth and love and the loss of them had been utterly devastating. Even so, there wasn't a day that went by when I wasn't grateful to have been brought up as I was.

Audrey gave me an approving look. 'Your sadness is leaking through a little, but only a touch. Your shields are good.'

'My shields?' I asked blankly.

She studied me. 'Emory said you had no knowledge of your empathy.'

I shook my head. 'None. I can't control it.'

'Oh but you do, rigidly. Not consciously, perhaps, but you do control it. An empath with no control quickly goes mad. Once they are introduced to the realm, they can feel emotions around them all the time and it is overwhelming.' She studied me. 'You must have already had good mental discipline before you were Introduced.'

I sat back heavily against the sofa. 'My mum,' I said wonderingly. 'She made me meditate every day when I was growing up. I still do – it's a habit. And my dad, he taught me breathing exercises for when I'm stressed.'

Audrey beamed as if a puzzle had been solved. 'That'd do it. What did your mother have you imagine?'

'The ocean, the beach.'

'Excellent. That's the most popular mental exercise. The sounds of the ocean drown out the "sounds" of the emotions around us, giving us a kind of white-noise protection.'

I had a lump in my throat. My mum had been protecting me my whole life in ways I'd had no idea about, and I couldn't talk to her about it or thank her for it. She protected me in every single way that she could, but she hadn't been able to protect me from the loss of her and Dad.

Audrey moved closer. 'Let it out, child. Grief is the echo of love. Honour it.' She wrapped an arm around me. 'Let it out, child.'

I disagreed with her but I couldn't fight the intent behind her words. All-consuming raw grief rushed over me and I started to cry so hard that I felt like I would never stop.

CHAPTER 9

M Y TEARS EVENTUALLY slowed. Normally after a crying jag I felt irritated with myself for being pulled down again, for being so vulnerable to this pain even after all these years. But now I just felt … cleansed. I took a deep breath and let it slowly out. In for four seconds, hold for seven seconds and out for eight seconds. It was a breathing technique Dad had taught me.

'They gave you all the tools you need. The ocean, the breath,' Audrey said.

I needed to move past this fragile moment. 'Tell me what to do. How to be an empath.'

'Child, you are an empath. To *be* – just let your heart beat. But how to hear the emotions around you? You need to listen.'

I frowned.

'You need to let the ocean's roar grow quiet,' she clarified, like it was obvious, like there was a mute button on the sea.

'And I do that how?' I asked, a tad impatiently.

'Everyone has different techniques. For me, I let the

tide go out. As the ocean recedes, so I can feel what is around me. It takes practice – and I don't suggest you start in a crowd. You must start small, with one other person only. With time and practice, you'll be able to get the ocean to recede in a moment and bring it back just as quickly. I often used it to feel a room, to see who was with me, who was angry, who was argumentative. It is a great skill for a leader.'

I snorted. 'I'm no leader,' I pointed out.

'No. But Emory is.'

I opened my mouth to protest. I was a PI, not some sort of fancy consort for Emory. But my outrage was warring with my insecurity. Maybe my empathy was the only reason Emory wanted me. I was pretty but I wasn't Elvira stunning yet he, king of the dragons, was dating me. Maybe he had an ulterior motive.

Audrey squeezed my hand. 'I've been an empath for centuries and my skills are like a Michelin-star chef compared to your fast-food cook. I can sense your outrage and your insecurity, but I can assure you that Emory isn't courting you for your skillset. He would only have brought you to me if he thought you were his mate. He wouldn't risk me for anyone else.'

'Risk you?'

'I am old, child. Older than I have a right to be.'

'I thought dragons were immortal?'

'Oh, some of us could live forever if we chose to, but

after innumerable centuries the tedium of life wears on you. To see loved ones go before their time, to see kingdoms rise and fall. To see the landscape being carved up and changed. Eventually we all chose to fade. Sharing my life with Cuth has accelerated the process. To give him a longer life span, I gave up my own. I don't regret it but our time is drawing near. Soon. It will be very soon. Even now I feel an ache in my bones, a fever in my skin. We have little time left.'

'Are you a seer, too?'

Audrey laughed a little. 'No, nothing so exalted.' She stood abruptly and walked to a bookshelf, selected a book and grabbed a bulging hessian sack that was resting on the floor. She handed the book to me and set down the sack down next to the sofa.

The tome was weighty and leatherbound. It was called *The Secret of Feeling*. I opened it reverently. The pages were old and the script was so curled and cursive that it was a struggle to read it.

'You may take it. Treat it well, it's even older than it looks.' Audrey nodded briskly. 'That concludes our lesson, Jessica Sharp.'

I blinked. 'What?'

'I have taught you all I can.'

My mouth dropped open; she had taught me nothing!

Her lips curved in a smile. 'You must learn by doing,

Jessica.' She turned to Gato. 'You know the time, Isaac?'

He barked.

'Good.' She picked up the hessian sack. 'I'd change as soon as you arrive. I was staying at The Fox and Hound pub.'

'Hold up – what—' I protested, then Gato touched his snout to my forehead and the house around us disappeared. We were in a darkened wood. Emory was gone, and so was the road we'd driven down.

I glared at Gato. 'What the hell? Which time have you sent us to?'

Gato ducked his head and tucked his tail between his legs. He wouldn't meet my gaze.

I'm pretty unshakeable, but a house can't be built in a day. For us to be in a time with no house, we'd moved back years.

I used my breathing techniques to grab some calm. Feeling steadier, I turned my attention to the sack in my hands. I opened it and looked inside. Oh hell, no! I pulled out a black dress with a full skirt. There was a stained white apron and a shawl. I stared at them. My best guess was that the clothes were Victorian.

'You better not have sent us into Victorian times!' I growled at Gato. He let out a low whine. 'Oh hell,' I muttered. I blew out a breath. 'Well, you can send us back anytime, right?'

Gato gave a wag but he still wouldn't look at me.

'There's no time like the present, I guess.' Nature was calling – too many mugs of tea – so I decided to attend to that first. Luckily this wasn't my first wee in a wood. Feeling a little more comfortable, if still rather over-whelmed, I stripped off my jeans and pulled on the outfit. Luckily the neckline was high so I could tuck the emerald pendant that Emory had given me safely out of sight.

I looked in the sack again: no shoes. The dress was so long that my feet weren't visible, which was useful because my black trainers would have stood out a mile away if anyone had seen them. I had no idea how Victorian women wore their hair, so I left it loose around my face.

In the bottom of the sack was a freshly baked loaf of bread and a canteen of water – well, I assumed it was water. Right then, I'd have been quite happy if it had turned out to be rum. I folded up my clothes but in the end left them on the damp earth. We were in the middle of the woods; if I didn't make it back, they'd probably degrade before someone found them.

I turned to Gato. 'What now?'

His tongue lolled out and he gave a doggy grin, then he started to grow. His eyes transformed to red as he grew and grew into what I affectionately call his 'battle-cat form'. When he was done, he was the size of a small horse. He moved over to a fallen log and looked at me patiently.

I immediately caught his meaning. 'You're kidding. I can't ride you!' I argued.

He stared back. He had a point: I had no transport and no clue where we were. I sighed. Fine. I grabbed the hessian bag and climbed onto the log. 'You'd better not spike me,' I groused.

I eyed his obsidian spikes with apprehension, but they instantly retracted as I ghosted a hand down them before reappearing again once my hand had passed over them. It would probably be fine. I grasped the fur on top of Gato's neck and did a little hop and jump onto his back. As I settled myself, the spikes remained retracted. I put the hessian sack on my lap then reached forwards and patted him. 'Okay,' I said, resigned to this insane situation. 'Let's go.'

Gato surged forwards, and I clung to him. Man, he could *move*. He broke into a run, but with no saddle and no idea of his stride I kept bouncing on his back on the off beat. I gritted my teeth and tried to settle into a more comfortable rhythm. After maybe ten minutes, I finally found my pace, and things got a little more comfortable.

We continued for a good forty minutes until we started to see signs of civilisation. First we saw farmhouses but then, as we moved closer to where I expected Liverpool to be, I saw signs of the city I knew. Gato stopped abruptly and I swung down off his back. He shifted back to dog form. I guessed it would be easier in the Common realm for him to appear as a dog rather than a horse. We both stayed in the Other.

We continued on foot. I had no idea of our destination but Gato seemed confident so I followed him. The houses now were coming thick and fast, crowded and overfilled. The stench was awful. Kids were fetching drinking water from a large fountain. A woman was pouring a bucket of waste into a gulley in the street. I grimaced at the splashback.

Gato kept us moving, taking us through a maze of long uphill streets and through cramped courtyards. It was winter but I could only see the odd fire lit in the cramped houses. One of the houses had its door open as I went by and I spied about a dozen occupants in its cramped quarters. Never had I been happier to be born in modern times.

I could see the docks in the distance but Gato led me away from them and deeper into the slums. I trailed along feeling out of place.

'Give us it back! It's mine!' a young boy shouted, pulling on a raggedy teddy. *True.* The boy was small – eight or nine, I guessed. The other boy was older, fourteen or fifteen. He was sneering, and he was pushing the little boy down. All the while, the kid kept a vice-like grip on the teddy.

I hate bullies in all their forms so I marched over with little thought. 'Let it go,' I ordered the teenager.

'And who are you? His ma?' The boy's lip curled up in a sneer. He had no fear and no respect.

I narrowed my eyes, but before I could argue with the brat Gato let out an horrific growl and stalked towards him. The lad let out a yelp and turned and ran away. Gato chased him merrily for a street or two before trotting back, tongue lolling. 'Good boy,' I greeted him, patting him again.

The little boy was still sprawled on the ground, holding his mucky teddy bear to his chest. I held out a hand to help him up. 'Are you all right?' I asked.

The boy met my eyes with his own bright-green ones and I stilled. My heart stopped for a beat. I knew those eyes.

Emory.

He frowned at me. 'How do you know my name?' His accent was Scouse, thick and broad, unlike the refined accent the present-day Emory often touted.

I blinked; I hadn't realised I had spoken aloud. 'I was sent here to help you,' I admitted.

He eyed me with suspicion. 'Sent by who? Ma and Pa are dead.'

'Does it matter? I have some food. Let's go somewhere and talk.'

He looked away from me as he considered then he reached out and stroked Gato, who sat happily and let him. It was noticeably at odds with the way Gato had acted when he first met adult Emory.

Emory gave Gato another stroke. Caution was warring with hunger and eventually hunger won. 'All right. This way.'

He led me down the narrow streets until he knocked on the front door of a terraced house. He knocked rhythmically and I guessed it was a code. There was no response so he pushed open the door. The downstairs consisted of a single room, no bigger than my kitchen. Clothes and belongings lay around it in small piles. A kids' flop, I guessed.

I sat on the floor; there was nowhere else. 'Where is everyone?' I asked.

'Out.' He shrugged. Chatty.

I reached into my hessian sack, pulled off a hunk of the loaf of bread and tossed it to Emory. He caught it easily and crammed most of it into his mouth. When he paused for breath, I passed him the canteen of water. He took a sip, and his nose wrinkled. 'Tastes funny,' he commented, but he took a few more gulps before handing it back to me. I drank a little to show him it was fine. Reassured, he settled back to his bread.

I knew that my empathy would be really handy right about now, and there was no better time to put Audrey's brief lessons into play. Cautiously, I imagined the ocean and its roar. Then I imagined the waves falling back and away, growing quieter and quieter. I started to feel an anxiety that I realised wasn't my own, as well as the faintest glimmer of hope. It was the hope that crushed me.

I didn't know how to do this but I'd give it my best shot. Emory needed to be introduced, to be told what he was. 'There's another world,' I said. 'One where magic exists.'

He rolled his eyes. 'Sure, and I'm a dragon.'

I grinned. Somehow he knew, even if he didn't know it. 'You are,' I agreed.

The glimmer of hope snuffed out and his anger rose. He thought I was teasing him. The fragile trust that had started to grow between us flickered and died.

I bit my lip. 'Watch,' I said.

I wanted the canteen of water to float, to rise up in the air. 'Up,' I ordered. The canteen flew up. Instead of feeling that I'd impressed him, I felt Emory's surprise followed by scorn. He thought it was a trick.

He reached above the canteen and felt all around it. 'Where are the ropes?' he asked finally.

'No ropes. Just magic,' I said. It would need something more convincing.

I wanted his teddy to be clean and fresh. 'Clean,' I intoned. His teddy instantly lost all its grubby marks. Emory's eyes widened, and I felt a cautious hope creep back in. 'You *are* a dragon,' I said. 'We just need to get you to your people, and they will introduce you to the

Other realm properly. I'm sorry I haven't done a very good job of it.'

'Who are you?' he asked. Disbelief was still his overriding emotion but he was willing to humour me.

'You can call me Jessica,' I offered.

'So where do we need to go?'

'Do you know a pub called The Fox and the Hound?'

'It's on the nice side of town.'

'Well, that's where we're going. Are you full, or would you like some more bread?'

I felt Emory's longing but he just shrugged. He was still hungry. 'I'm fine,' he muttered.

My heart squeezed. I reached into my bag and pulled off a huge hunk of bread. 'Here you go,' I said softly.

He snatched it quickly, like he was scared I'd change my mind. I wanted desperately to hug him but I knew it would be hugely inappropriate; he didn't know me from Eve, even if I knew him. I offered him the canteen again and he drank from it several times before handing it back. His movements were quick and sudden and he often pulled back, looking at me from behind his greasy hair. He was tense, waiting for the other shoe to drop. He *wanted* to believe me, but he still couldn't.

We waited until he'd eaten enough then we set off, Emory leading the way. Gradually the streets widened and the stench lessened. The houses grew cleaner and tidier, and the clothes grew finer. 'One day,' Emory muttered, glaring at a hoity-toity couple who looked at us disdainfully.

'One day,' I agreed. 'One day you'll be richer than all of them.'

He flashed me a grin and for a moment I could see the self-assured man he would become. It reassured me; deep down my Emory was there, waiting to be nurtured.

Emory led us down a smaller side street. 'Not long now,' he said, then abruptly he froze. Four men appeared in front of him, each one incredibly well dressed and incredibly handsome. Vampyrs.

The front man sneered. 'Well now, look what we have here! A hatchling and his mama a little too far from the nest.'

Feeling nothing but rage and hatred, I muted the ocean then I let it roar again. I didn't have time to second-guess myself. 'Protect Emory!' I yelled at Gato.

I reached into my sack and prayed that Glimmer could move across time as well as space. Nope. Fuck.

I dropped the sack to free my hands and thought desperately. I let out a sharp breath. I had magic, dammit. I'd primed air before and I could do it again.

I gathered my intention. I wanted the wind to push them over, I wanted the air to grow into a huge gust of wind they couldn't withstand. Exhaling sharply, I ordered, 'Grow.'

The wind gathered until it whipped around us, blowing my hair into my face so I could barely see. 'Go!' I commanded the tumultuous air, throwing it at the vampyrs.

It was a strong wind, though not quite a hurricane. It wasn't the dramatic Dorothy-like tornado I'd been hoping for but it would do as a distraction. The vampyrs grabbed onto anything around them to stop themselves falling over.

Gato had transformed once again into his battle-cat form. I grabbed Emory and threw him onto my hellhound's back. 'Run!' I yelled. I held the wind on the vampyrs as we pushed through them.

I hadn't thought this through. I was having to fight through the wind, and it was affecting me almost as much as them. I consciously directed the wind to lessen around me. As we moved beyond the vampyrs, I focused the wind back on them and held it for as long as I could. When they were out of sight, I felt the magic drop. I'd lost my focus.

I swore loudly. 'Keep running!' I ordered Gato. Emory was clinging to his back, bouncing around as we fled. Dignity be damned; I lifted the full skirts of my dress and ran. Dimly it crossed my mind to be thankful I was wearing my trainers.

We ran down another small street and the vampyrs phased out of the shadows ahead of us. They just wouldn't quit. There was a sign hanging from a wooden post that proclaimed the shop to be a barber's. I needed that post; I needed it to fly out of the ground into my hand. 'Come!' The wooden post surged up from the ground. As I grasped it, I immediately stumbled under its weight. Dammit, I couldn't fight like this. I needed it to be light and manoeuvrable but still pack a punch when I swung it 'Lighter!' Instantly the wood felt lighter.

One of the vampyrs came towards me, sneering and confident of his abilities. He was in for a shock because I was no Victorian damsel. I knew he could move fast, so I started my roundhouse kick before he came at me. I timed it perfectly; as he moved into my path, my foot collided with his head and he careened back, slamming into the wall. Lights out.

I hefted my makeshift club and was swinging it before the second vampyr came at me. He blocked me, and I felt a surge of panic. As we both clung onto the wood, he swung me into a wall with a solid crunch. I winced as something cut into my left arm. I was in trouble. I needed to think outside of the box but my mind was floundering, stuck in panic and pain.

Inspiration struck. 'Flames!' I shouted.

The vampyr dropped the wood in panic, expecting it to combust. He didn't realise I'd been bluffing; I didn't have any affinity with fire so I couldn't summon it without a primer – but apparently my opponent didn't know that.

It gave me the momentary advantage that I needed. The vampyr snarled at me when no flames materialised. I swung the pole again as he leapt towards me, and this time I hit true. His head made a satisfying thunk as it collided with the wood. Blood pooled down his right temple and he slid to the floor, eyes wide and unseeing. I didn't get time to freak out that I might have killed him. Anyway, he was already dead so how *could* I kill him?

Two were down but another vampyr had phased into the fray; they just wouldn't quit. We needed to reach the pub.

Gato leapt forwards with Emory still on his back and used his jaws to rip through the throat of the closest vampyr. I moved to the next one and hefted my make-shift weapon higher. Just as I was about to swing at him, I froze. It was Wokeshire.

'Wokeshire, stop!' I shouted. Thankfully, he paused. 'You must stop, Lord Wokeshire! If you kill me, I can't save Mererid one day,' I explained urgently.

He blinked. 'I'm not Lord Wokeshire,' he said finally. 'That is.' He pointed to one of bodies on the floor. We both stared at it for a moment and then it disintegrated into dust.

'I'm promoting you,' I said flatly. 'And one day we'll meet again, and I'll save your daughter's life. I promise you. But you must let me and the boy get away today so I can save you tomorrow.'

'You're a seer.'

'Something like that,' I agreed. 'Let us go.'

He hesitated and I took the opportunity to break into a run again. Gato, Emory and I careened around the corner. I was no longer sure if we were being pursued or not, but my heart was hammering, and adrenalin was surging through me.

'Are you all right? Are you hurt?' I asked Emory frantically. I tried to check him over as I ran but I couldn't see any injuries.

'I'm fine, ma'am,' he panted, eyes wide.

I frowned. 'Damn vampyrs. Are we close to the pub?'

'Just around this corner,' he assured me. Then, 'Vampyrs,' he breathed, his voice full of awe.

We turned a corner and burst into a square. The pub was at the far side, and outside there were a number of people and horse-drawn carts milling around. The people were dressed in black; I hoped they were brethren and not more vampyrs. Or they could just be normal Commoners; black was the standard colour, it seemed.

We slowed to a walk. Our arrival had been noted as we approached the tavern. I had no idea what time it was but the sky was starting to darken. I needed to get Emory to safety before the vampyrs came back in force. Nightfall was their hunting time.

There must have been fifteen or twenty people outside the pub, organising and loading the carts. In the middle were a couple I instantly recognised. Audrey's auburn hair was threaded with silver and her face was lined; she younger, yes, but it was undoubtedly her. Cuthbert's full head of hair was black and shaggy, his face was craggy but his eyes were the same. It was definitely them.

Relief poured through me, but we weren't out of the woods yet. There was a shout and a snarl from behind me. I pulled Emory off Gato's back. 'Protect us!' I barked at Gato as I ran towards the centre of the group dressed in black. All eyes were on me, but the crowd parted to let us in.

I looked back and saw five vampyrs standing at the edge of the square. Gato was in front of them, spikes raised and growling ferociously.

I wrapped an arm around Emory and drew him with me. 'Prime!' I called out.

'Yes?' Cuthbert responded, raising an eyebrow.

I rolled my eyes. 'If a woman can be queen, she can be Prime.'

'Indeed,' Audrey said with a smirk. 'She can.'

'We're being pursued by vampyrs. This is Emory. He hasn't been Introduced yet but he's a dragon. He's an orphan. Will you help us?'

Audrey smiled warmly at Emory. 'Of course.' *True.* She walked to the edge of the group and raised her voice to the vampyrs lingering in the darkness. 'Too slow, old boys, too slow. He is mine now. Come and get him if you dare.'

I did a face palm. Was it necessary to goad them?

'Keep him today,' one of the vampyrs called back. 'We'll get him another day. We'll get you all, one hatchling at a time, until you're nothing but a memory.'

Audrey smirked. 'It's nice to see that even in death you can still hold onto your dreams. But that's all they will ever be. We will crush you into the dust that you always become.'

'We'll see,' the vampyr responded, glaring.

'Indeed we shall.'

The lead vampyr jerked his head, and the others started to phase away. I looked up and met Wokeshire's eyes. 'Mererid,' he mouthed at me. I nodded. I'd live up to my vow – after all, I'd already done it. Wokeshire melted into the shadows and all of the vampyrs were gone.

I let out a sharp breath of relief and hugged Emory. 'You're safe now. She'll help you,' I told him earnestly. 'I promise.' And, because I could, I silenced the ocean for a moment. I felt his uncertainty, his unwillingness to trust, but through it that thread of hope. 'If you don't like it, you can always run away,' I whispered.

'To you?' he asked in a small voice, and my heart broke a little.

'Yes,' I said firmly. 'You can always run to me.'

CHAPTER 10

G ATO TROTTED AWAY, presumably to make sure the vampyrs really were gone. We were lucky: we had caught Audrey and Cuthbert in the nick of time. They were moving tonight to a new location. Another day and I would have missed them. There would have been no saving Emory, a thought that made my stomach churn.

The carts were loaded, and Audrey and Cuthbert climbed into one, gesturing for Emory to join them. Still he hesitated.

'They're going to take such good care of you,' I promised again. 'You'll be fine.' I tried to smile reassuringly. He was about to be raised by uber-traditional dragons, who in modern times would still fight against phones and modern technology though Emory would embrace them. I bit my lip, but in the end I decided to give him a shove in the right direction. 'Remember, tradition is important but so is moving with the times,' I said. 'Great change is coming. It's far easier to ride the wave than resist it.'

Emory nodded, though I wasn't sure if he understood what I meant. I was crap at analogies He probably hadn't gone surfing before – hell, he probably hadn't even gone swimming.

His frame was so skeletal, and he was so small. I couldn't help giving him another quick hug. My every nurturing instinct was shouting at me to look after him but that wasn't my role in Emory's life. Not yet, anyway. I looked into his emerald-green eyes. 'Be brave. You can do it. You'll rise above them all.'

He gave a tremulous smile, but I still saw self-doubt. I couldn't give him that belief; he would have to build it himself.

'Every dragon needs some treasure.' I unfastened the pendant around my neck and fastened it around his. 'Your first piece.'

Emory's mouth dropped, eyes wide as he stared at the jewel around his neck.

Gato trotted up to us carrying Emory's teddy bear carefully in his mouth. I felt a surge of affection for my hound. He knew how important the toy was. I took the bear from Gato's maw and handed it to Emory. His eyes filled with unshed tears and he clasped it to his heart. 'Your *second* piece,' I corrected softly, because I had no doubt that the teddy bear was the most important treasure of all.

'Go on now.' I pushed him towards the cart. He climbed in but straight away turned to watch me.

Audrey nodded solemnly at me. The driver gave a

click to the horses and the cart lurched forwards. Emory held my gaze until they disappeared out of sight.

Darkness had fallen, and there were still some rogue vampyrs out there, as well as other things that go bump in the night. 'Will you be okay if I ride you again?' I asked Gato.

He gave me a flat look which I took to be an 'of course'. I climbed on his back and we set off. 'Faster,' I urged. 'Let's go.'

He took me at my word and surged forwards. This time it didn't take me too long to find my rhythm. We moved through the cobbled streets, avoiding people as much as possible, and it wasn't long before we broke out of the reaches of the city. I felt happier in the countryside. We weren't too far now from the woods and Audrey and Cuthbert's present-day retreat.

Darkness had descended, but the moon was high, lighting our way. Eventually we reached the clearing where my clothing was lying, still neatly folded. I guess I hadn't needed to worry about it decomposing. I slid off Gato's back and picked it up.

'Take us back, pup,' I commanded softly. I was tired and my arm was aching. The adrenalin had stopped coursing through me, leaving me weary. I wanted to see adult Emory and reassure myself that he was all right, that leaving him with Audrey and Cuthbert had been the right choice.

Gato stood on his hind legs and touched his nose to my forehead. He shifted us through the Third Realm, the world flashed and suddenly Audrey and Cuthbert's house was there. The lights were blazing; night had fallen here too. Time had passed for Emory while I had been away. I hoped he hadn't been too worried about my sudden absence, and I wondered what Audrey had told him.

I knocked on the door. Almost instantly Emory flung it open. He started to speak but his words died as he took in my attire and he paled. His mouth remained open.

'You've grown,' I said drily.

That spurred him into action. He pulled me into his arms and held me tightly. 'I thought you were her descendant,' he admitted. 'You looked so like her that it took my breath away the first time I saw you. But then I realised she was human – she couldn't possibly have lived long enough to be you. I thought you were the great-great-great-something of the woman who saved me. But it was you.'

'It was me,' I agreed. I hugged him back. 'Was it right? To leave you with Audrey and Cuthbert?'

He drew back and beamed at me. 'Yes, it was right. It was home.'

My eyes filled with tears and I nodded, speechless as relief flooded through me.

'Let the poor girl in,' came Audrey's strident command from the lounge.

Emory obediently stepped back and let me into the warmth. I sighed softly. Man, I love central heating. I kicked off my trainers and this time, Cuthbert didn't stop me.

There was a fire burning in the lounge, and Gato wasted no time in going to lie in front of it. He deserved to bask in the warmth. I checked the time: 8 p.m. No wonder I was hungry.

I looked down at my clothes and grimaced. There was blood on me, probably vampyrs', possibly mine. 'Would you mind if I shower?' I asked Audrey.

'Not at all. I'll show you to the spare room. Take your time. We've food for you, but it will keep.' Audrey heaved herself up and walked carefully down a corridor to a bedroom. As she passed me some towels, she turned to me with a serious expression on her face.

'Be considerate of Emory. He has just found out that you are the single most influential person in his life. You rescued him, saved him from the slums and the vampyrs, and delivered him to his foster family. He may be a little over-zealous in his care for you but grin and bear it. He needs to find his ground again.' She was lecturing me like any mother protective of her son. It made me happy.

She touched my arm affectionately. 'I'm glad to have met you, Jessica Sharp. It does my heart good to see Emory so happy. I can relax now.'

I smiled wanly. She and Cuthbert seemed determined

to pair us up, and I didn't have it in me to argue. Not when I wasn't sure which way things might go.

Audrey showed me how the shower functioned and left me to it. I had never been happier to shower. The wound in my left arm wasn't too bad, only a puncture that had ripped a little. Perhaps the vampyr had impaled me on a nail or something. I was pretty sure I was up to date with my tetanus. I dressed, leaving the injury to the open air to dry. It had stopped bleeding, and I was less concerned about it now that I'd seen it.

I was hungry and tired in that order, so I made my way back to the lounge. Emory stood up as I walked in. His eyes flicked over me anxiously and he frowned as he saw the mark on my arm. 'You're injured,' he said darkly. 'I didn't know you were injured.' He crossed the distance between us with vampiric speed, leant down and gently licked the injury.

I giggled. 'That tickles!' I complained.

'It heals,' Emory countered. 'So suck it up.' He licked me again a few times for good measure. When he drew back the wound was gone, and not even a scar remained.

'Cool. It's a lot quicker than getting a witch to cover you in runic gunk,' I said.

Emory frowned. 'When did you get hurt so badly you needed a witch?'

'When I released a horde of Ronan's unicorns from captivity. It happened before you were around.'

'No more releasing any animals which you have to define using the term "horde".'

'You have all of these rules.'

'Only a few. For example, always ride the wave.' He tucked a stray strand of hair behind my ear. 'Let's get you fed.'

He led me to the sofas. Audrey and Cuthbert were sitting together, leaning affectionately against each other. Emory sat me down and returned a moment later with a huge tray of food. 'I wasn't sure what you'd want. It's getting a bit late for a full dinner, but I can get you a hot option if you want.' The tray had crackers and cheese, grapes, mango and banana. It had huge chunks of fresh bread slathered with butter and some with pâté. It was very much like the bread I had given to Emory nearly two centuries earlier.

My mouth watered. 'This is great. Thank you.'

Emory laid the tray on the coffee table and pulled out a side plate. He sat down on the floor, between me and the coffee table, and prepared some cheese and crackers for me. He passed me the plate and watched quietly while I ate.

Cuthbert clicked on some relaxing acoustic tunes, and he and Audrey talked quietly. When my side plate was empty, Emory took it wordlessly and filled it for me again. Each time I handed back the plate, he gave me something new.

Finally I held up my hand. 'I'm full now,' I assured him. Emory stood and picked up the tray. 'Come on,' Emory said, whistling to Gato. 'You're my hero too. Best get you fed.'

As Gato trotted happily after him, Emory ruffled his head. 'Thanks for the ride, pup.' The affection in his tone warmed me. After a few minutes, he came back with a pot of tea and a tray of mugs. He served us all and settled on the sofa next to me.

'Thank you for taking care of me,' I murmured. It felt strange to be looked after. As a committed feminist, I found it hard to let myself be waited on. I believed in equality of the genders; having him run around after me was just odd. If I hadn't had Audrey's warning, I probably would have resisted his attempts to serve me, but I got the feeling that he needed to do it.

Audrey and Cuthbert started to tell me tales of Emory's childhood, his first transformation, his first prank. We stayed up until the small hours laughing together. As the night wore on, Audrey transformed into her dragon form to stretch out. Cuthbert lay against her and my brain clicked. I knew where I'd seen them before – with my parents in a photograph in Conrad's house.

'You knew my parents,' I blurted out.

Audrey's great head swung towards me. 'Yes, we knew George and Mary.' A yawn cracked her face and her great maw swung open, exposing row after row of razor-sharp teeth. 'We were friends. I'll happily tell you more about them, but tomorrow perhaps. It's time for us to retire.'

I wanted to argue but I was just as shattered, so I nodded. Tomorrow would come soon enough. I could hardly keep my eyes open as Emory and I retired to the spare room. Gato collapsed on the floor beside us with a humph. I shrugged off my jeans and slid into the bed, still with my T-shirt and my knickers on. Emory stripped down to his silk boxers, climbed in next to me and pulled me close for a cuddle.

I was too tired to feel weird about sleeping with Emory. Wrapped in his warmth, I cautiously let the ocean recede. All I could feel was love.

CHAPTER II

A STAB OF panic shot through me, waking me abruptly. It was enough to jolt me upright and I looked around in confusion, my heart beating wildly. I realised that I had slept all night with the ocean sounds silenced, and my mental shields were still down. The panic that I felt wasn't my own but Emory's. I hauled the covers back and ran to where I could feel he was.

Audrey and Cuthbert were both slumped over the dining-room table. They'd laid out breakfast and then it looked like they'd passed out. Emory pulled Audrey out of her chair, cradled her carefully and laid her down. 'She's burning up.' His voice was laced with panic.

Gato padded over on quiet feet. As he laid down next to Audrey and rested his head on her tummy, he let out a soft whine.

'I'll get a cool flannel,' I said, but first I went over to Cuthbert. 'He's hot, too.' He was heavy, but gravity was on my side as I carefully manoeuvred him out of his chair and laid him down.

Emory already had his phone out. 'I need a helicopter

now at the former Prime's residence – transport to the hospital. This is need-to-know only,' he said sharply, rattling off the secret co-ordinates. He must have received an affirmative because he hung up.

I dashed back to our bedroom and held two flannels under the cold tap, squeezed out the excess moisture and carried them back. 'If this is the virus, how come Cuthbert is affected?' I was thinking aloud. 'He's human. No humans have been affected that we know of.'

'He's mated to Audrey,' Emory muttered, not taking his eyes off her.

'So?'

'So they're linked. His extended life span is linked to hers. If she's dying, so is he.'

We worked in silence to cool them down. Because they were unconscious, it was difficult to get them to swallow liquid but Emory insisted that we try. Dehydration had been a big issue for the youngling dragon who was sick. We poured small amounts of water into their mouths, barely a spoonful at a time, and they swallowed reflexively. It was better than nothing. We continued until we heard the sounds of the helicopter arriving. Finally.

Emory looked up. 'You'd better get dressed.'

I started. Shit. I was still in knickers and a T-shirt. I bolted for the bedroom before the helicopter landed in front of the glass-walled lounge.

I dressed hastily. When I went back into the room, the wide French doors were open. Two helicopters had landed, one for Audrey and one for Cuthbert, who had both been placed on stretchers. Emory kept moving between them, touching their hands and talking to them even though they were unconscious. My heart ached for him; I knew what it was like to lose your parents, and Audrey and Cuthbert were undoubtedly the nearest thing to parents that Emory had. His worry pervaded his every motion.

When Audrey and Cuthbert were safely loaded up, Emory returned with another man whom I vaguely recognised from Conrad's house. He was one of the brethren, a hulking man, all solid muscle. I guessed that being raised around dragons, you'd want some strength of your own. For such a large man, he moved lightly on his feet. Military training, I surmised.

Emory pulled me into a hug. 'I'm sorry, I have to go with them. I need to see them safe.'

'Of course! I'll speak with Jack and see if I can meet with Catriona again. And I'll speak to Hes about how far they got digging into Catriona's life.'

Emory stepped back and gestured to the huge man beside him. 'This is Tom Smith, my second. He can update you – he was with Hes. Tom is going to help you while I'm at the hospital.'

I didn't want to cause a scene, not with Audrey and

Cuthbert so ill and Emory being so upset, but... I frowned. 'I don't need a bodyguard.'

'I know you don't,' Emory assured me. 'But I'm hiring you officially to look into who or what is causing this illness so you need more manpower. Use Tom. He's useful.' That assuaged my prickly independence because all of it rang *true*.

I swallowed any further objections. Now wasn't the time, that was for sure, and I wasn't one to look a gift horse in the mouth. Emory was right: extra manpower was always useful. 'Okay. Go,' I said. 'Let me know how they get on.' I didn't tell him that Audrey had said her time was near. I hoped she was wrong.

I was also kicking myself for not pressing the issue about my parents. What if Audrey and Cuthbert knew something about their deaths, or what had sent them into hiding? If Emory's foster parents died, I might lose a piece of the puzzle forever. I knew it was selfish to be concerned, but my parents' deaths had been an all-consuming mystery for me for years, a constant nagging thorn in my side. For Emory's sake I hoped with all my heart that Audrey and Cuthbert would recover – and for my own sake, too.

Emory turned to go to the helicopters but then turned back and crossed the distance between us. He pulled me to him and kissed me, his tongue invading my mouth forcefully and passionately. My heart rate shot up, and my mind switched off. When he finally pulled away, his eyes were dark. 'Stay safe, Jessica Sharp.' His tone was oddly formal.

'You too,' I managed.

He walked away and climbed into the helicopter with Audrey and I watched them set off. As the noise receded, I looked around the room. Breakfast still covered the table: toast and boiled eggs. I didn't have any appetite, but there was no point in it going to waste.

I turned to Gato. 'Who's a lucky boy? A nice breakfast for you.' I fetched some of his dry food from the car, mixed in the leftovers and Gato happily swallowed it all down. I washed the dishes, straightened up the house and packed my things. After a moment's hesitation, I took the Victorian clothes. Maybe they'd be good as a costume one day, or maybe I was just getting sentimental.

All packed up, I went into the lounge where Tom was standing silently. 'Do you have a key to lock up with?' I asked.

'Yes, ma'am,' he confirmed.

'Ugh, not ma'am. Call me Jinx, please.'

He hesitated. 'Jinx,' he said finally.

'Let's go. I'll ring Jack when we're on the road.'

We loaded up and squeezed into the tiny Ford Focus. Emory was right, maybe I did need a bigger car. Or smaller passengers. Emory had texted me Jack's number, so I waited until I was on the road before I dialled him hands free. 'Yes?' he answered.

'Jack? It's Jinx.'

'Hey, Jinx. How are you?'

'I'm okay. Listen, can I see Catriona again today? I've been working on my empathy. I'm not promising anything, but I can at least try.'

He blew out a breath of relief. 'Yes please. She's in the Other ward in Arrowe Park Hospital.'

I blinked. 'There's an Other ward?'

'Yeah, though to be honest it's rarely used. Most people use their own medical providers. But cross-over staff work at the ward there, mostly junior witches and wizards who are still trying to make a name for themselves to start their own healing practices. The hospital has some advantages, though. Some problems need real medicine, like stitches and blood transfusions. Magic is great, but occasionally technology has its benefits.'

'When shall I come?'

'Visiting starts in a couple of hours at 10 a.m. Come then.'

I checked the time; it was still only 8 a.m. The helicopters had arrived quickly. 'Great, see you around.' I hung up. Next, I dialled Hes.

'Hey, Jinx,' she answered.

'Hey, Hes. You at my house?'

'Yeah. I hope that's okay.'

I rolled my eyes. 'Of course it is. I wanted to touch

base about your research on Catriona. I'll be home in twenty.'

'I'll put the kettle on,' Hes promised and rang off.

Tom and I drove in silence. I had a lot on my mind and so did he. From what I knew, there was an illness or virus out there that was affecting only the 'creature' denizens of the realm such as trolls, mermaids and dragons. We needed more information.

I picked up my phone again and dialled Shirdal.

'Jinx! How lovely to hear from you.' He was slurring, even though it was barely 8:20 a.m. Either he was still going from the night before or he was putting it on. He loved to be underestimated. My money was on the latter.

'It's not a chit-chat call,' I said sternly. 'I need you, quick sharp.'

'I need you, Sharp,' he purred back, his voice heavy with innuendo.

I rolled my eyes even though he couldn't see me. 'Yeah, yeah. Emory isn't here to hear it, so cut it out.'

Shirdal laughed. 'I have missed you, Jinx.' *True.* All traces of intoxication were gone.

I was mildly flattered, and I guessed it was kind of true for me too. The drunk griffin was *fun* – when he wasn't murdering or maiming. 'Back at you, big guy. I have some questions if you have time.'

'I've got lots of answers for you, Jinx.' Still mildly flirtatious.

'Have any of your griffins got sick?' I asked, cutting straight to the chase.

There was a heavy pause. 'Yes,' he admitted finally. 'A couple of our youngest, Charlize and Fergal.' I recognised the names; one of them had killed Reggie Evergreen, although I still didn't know which. I had let it go; they were assassins and Reggie's death was a business transaction. It mattered little who pulled the trigger, or in this case slashed their claws, it was the person who gave the order who was important. That had been Ronan, a piper and head of a drug cartel.

'Where are they?' I asked.

'They're in Arrowe, in the Other ward.'

'Do you know of any other creatures that are ill?'

'Early indicators are there's a Noah's Ark theme going on. It strikes in twos. Two dryads are in hospital. Two young griffins, two young trolls, two young dragons.'

'Only one mermaid,' I pointed out.

'Then you haven't found the other mermaid yet,' Shirdal suggested. 'Will you be coming to Arrowe later?' His question was deliberately light and airy.

Alarm bells rang. 'Maybe,' I fudged. 'I've got other things to do first.'

'Well give me a call if you're heading there, and I'll make sure I can meet you to smooth things over.'

'Any werewolves sick?' I demanded.

'No, but they're on the human side. This seems to be

a creatures-only illness.'

My gut was speaking to me, and I bit my lip. 'The lab that Ronan set up was developing something other than Boost, right?'

There was a heavy pause. 'Right,' Shirdal confirmed slowly. 'Though I didn't see inside the lab. The Connection minions were all talking about it.'

'Thanks. I'll drop you a message if I go to Arrowe.' *Lie.*

'Later, sweetheart.' He rang off.

Tom was looking at me with interest. 'You don't want him to know you're going to Arrowe?'

I shook my head. 'He's hiding something from me.'

Tom raised an eyebrow. 'And you know that how?'

'I guess gut instinct counts for a lot.' I carefully let the ocean sounds recede, partly because I could and partly because I was curious. Tom was feeling interest and curiosity, with a fair amount of caution thrown in. Fair enough. I wanted to tell him that the caution wasn't warranted; in this crazy realm I was as dangerous as a turtle unless I had Glimmer with me, and even then I was only up to lion standard. I felt in my jacket pocket. Empty. Turtle it was.

We pulled up to my house and Tom got out with me. Hes swung open the door. 'Hi, Tom!' she greeted him warmly.

'Hester.' He gave her a small smile.

Gato peed on my rosebush in the front garden and trotted in. True to her word, Hes had made a pot of tea. She grabbed an extra mug for Tom, and we sat in the lounge. I turned to her. 'Give me the rundown on Catriona.'

She was sitting to attention; this had been her first snooping job, albeit with Tom along from the ride. Nervously she flipped open her notebook.

'Catriona Barnes, aged twenty. She was employed as a barmaid at Walkabout. She earned good money in tips. Her co-workers describe her as fun, outgoing and flirtatious. She pulled her weight and she'd often volunteer for extra shifts. She was a keen sailor and went regularly to West Kirby Marina with friends.

'She went missing after a shift at work but no one reported it. The boss is a bitch, and it isn't unusual for people to throw the towel in without giving notice. The other staff assumed she'd had enough and walked out. That was about two months ago.

'Catriona's flatmate, Bonnie Adams, said she was a good housemate but that they kept largely to themselves. Bonnie is studying law at Liverpool and spends most of her spare time at the library. She got on well with Catriona, but they were like ships in the night. Catriona was clean and considerate; she'd buy a new pint of milk if they ran out. Bonnie saw her so rarely that she couldn't pinpoint when she went missing. The rent and utilities were paid by direct debit so Bonnie wasn't overly concerned. She just figured Catriona had skipped town.'

Hes flipped over the page. 'With Bonnie's permission, we searched Catriona's room. There were no signs of drugs or illegal activities. Her clothes were freshly laundered, no dirty ones in the hamper. Her reading style…' Hes blushed '…was a little – spicy.'

'Whips and chains, voyeurism, role play, group sex?' I asked, mostly to see Hes's reaction.

Her blush deepened. 'Yes. All of those.' She didn't meet Tom's eyes.

'So we might need to check out some sex clubs,' I said matter of factly. 'Any signs that this went further than light reading?'

'There were some leather outfits in the wardrobe,' Hes admitted. 'But they could have been sexy workwear for extra tips.'

'No gimp masks in the cupboard?'

Hes couldn't get any redder. 'Nope.'

'Anything else jump out at you?'

Hes shook her head. 'Most of her friends were from work or from the sailing club. She had a calendar on her wall counting down the days until her twenty-first birthday. It was last marked off on November 13th.'

'What happens when she hits twenty-one?' I mused.

'She gets to return home,' Tom offered.

I blinked. 'She can't finish shore leave early?'

He shook his head. 'No, the deal is they have to spend a full year away.'

'With no support?' I frowned. That seemed harsh. Even kids at uni could come home whenever they liked.

'They have the rest of the purse.'

'The purse?' I asked, wishing I didn't have to.

'A small group of mermaids. A bigger group is called a shoal.'

'So when they go on shore leave, it's with a purse?' Tom nodded. 'Are they supposed to stick together?' I asked.

'I don't know,' Tom admitted.

'That's something to speak to Jack about. Anything in your observations that Hes hasn't mentioned?'

'Catriona reads raunchy, but she has a huge bar of chocolate in her bedside table,' Tom replied. 'And ice cream in the fridge. I read it that she's single.'

'You don't think she's visiting sex clubs and hooking up?'

Tom shook his head again. 'No condoms, no pills, no potions.'

That distracted me for a moment. 'There's an anti-pregnancy potion?'

He shifted and looked embarrassed. His pale skin warmed. Ah yes: he thought I was having sex with his boss. Right.

'There's a weekly potion,' he said finally. 'Males or

females can take it. It's incredibly expensive and tastes foul. Most people stick to … other methods.'

Discussing contraception with Emory's second in command was fun. I took a great deal of delight in embarrassing hardened military types. My phone beeped, interrupting my teasing session before it really got started. It was a message from my friend and computer expert, Mo: *I've found him. He's visiting Arrowe Park Hospital now. No ward details yet – sorry.*

I stared at my phone, willing my poker face to stay in place. Bastion, my parent's killer, was at Arrowe Park Hospital. No wonder Shirdal wanted me to message him first. I stood. 'It's time to go to the hospital.'

'What did the message say?' Hes asked.

'That it's time to go,' I repeated sharply. 'Move.'

CHAPTER 12

I DECIDED TO take Gato with us, stuffed him into a doggy high-vis jacket and grabbed one for myself as well. Nothing guarantees invisibility like a high-vis jacket. Yes, the irony of that was not lost on me.

Hes went to the toilet before we left and I had to stop myself from snarling impatiently at her. This was my one opportunity to talk to Bastion. Mo had been trying to track my parent's assassin for weeks and this was the only blip on the radar so far. I couldn't miss him now because my assistant had a small bladder.

I climbed into the car, mentally visualised the ocean and practised my breathing exercises. I let the ocean sounds wash over me. When the passenger door slid shut, I had a grasp on my cool again. 'Buckle up,' I said to Hes and Tom. They both fastened their seatbelts.

I started the car and told myself firmly to drive sensibly. Getting pulled over for speeding wouldn't help me reach Bastion any faster. It was twenty minutes to Arrowe, so I decided to make another call I'd been putting off. Hopefully it would distract me from the urge to drive like a bat out of hell. I put the call through the hands free.

'Hey, Jinx. I'm glad you called.' Stone's voice was warm and rather too affectionate for my liking. I'd made it clear where we stood, or so I thought.

'Hey, Stone. I need a favour.'

He sighed. 'Sure you do. You know, I never thought I'd miss you calling me Rocky.'

'I'll call you Basalt again, if you like,' I offered lightly.

He snorted. 'No, I'm good. What do you need?'

'Ronan. He was running a lab, and he was cooking something other than Boost. What was it?'

'I haven't seen the final reports,' Stone admitted. *True.* 'I was pulled onto a new case – rogue elementals.'

I wanted to get the lowdown on the elementals, most-ly because I'm insanely nosy, but first I had to focus on Ronan. 'You didn't read the final reports but you read the interim ones,' I stated confidently. Stone had omitted to tell me a few things our first time around, and I was more wary now. His phraseology was important; he was always careful – too careful – not to lie to me.

'Yeah,' he admitted heavily. 'I read the interim ones. I can't say for sure, and I shouldn't say at all, but the initial conclusion was that he was manufacturing a virus.' *True.*

'A virus? Why?'

'There was a paper trail, a lot of money to an account in the Caymans. Last I heard, they hadn't tracked down whoever had paid it into the account. Leave it with me, and I'll do some digging.' *True.*

I didn't trust Stone like I once had, but I was confident he wasn't a bad person. He took his role as the Connection's enforcer seriously and he thought of himself as a representative of law and order. I was fairly confident he wasn't on the wrong side in this affair. He favoured the direct approach; he wouldn't poison anyone, he'd lop off their head.

'Some of the magical creatures have been getting sick,' I said finally.

'I'll dig into it,' Stone repeated. 'You stay out of it,' he ordered.

Funny thing: I don't do well with orders. 'Tell me about the elementals.' One order deserved another.

'Not much to tell. Someone keeps starting fires.'

'What does Benedict have to say about that?' I asked.

There was a beat of silence. 'And how do you know about Benedict?'

'Everyone knows Benedict is the head of the fire elementals,' I said breezily. Or at least Roscoe and Maxwell did.

'Steer clear of Benedict, he's not … stable,' Stone warned. I felt like he'd substituted 'stable' for 'sane' at the last minute.

'Mh-mm.' I made noises of agreement.

'Benedict swears it's not the work of an elemental,'

Stone confirmed.

'What makes you think it's an elemental rather than your everyday Common arsonist?'

'A few things. Firstly, all of the sites that were burnt down have been Other businesses. There's also been no evidence of an accelerant, yet all of these fires have been devastating. We haven't ruled out another perpetrator – a creature, perhaps.'

It struck me that he said creature rather than wizard. Wizards could prime fire, so why weren't they on the list? 'Or a wizard who primes fire?' I pointed out.

'Or a dragon,' Stone countered, his voice low.

I didn't like what he was insinuating. 'Bye, Stone.' I hung up.

Hes let out a whistle. 'He's not going to like you hanging up on him. He's still got it bad for you.'

I didn't respond. I didn't think she was wrong. Next I dialled Nate. 'Jinx,' he responded.

'Hey, Nate.' I saw Tom tense next to me. Ah yes: vampyrs and dragons didn't get on. Apparently, this extended to the mysterious brethren. 'Any vampyrs sick?' I asked.

'No, the undead remain annoyingly healthy,' Nate said lightly. 'But I've heard that even the gnomes have had some sickness. Dryads, dragons, trolls. I heard a rumour two ogres have been sick as well, but that's not been confirmed.'

'Witches, wizards, seers, elementals, werewolves?'

'No,' Nate said seriously. 'Anything on the human side has remained unaffected.'

'Untargeted,' I muttered tightly. 'Okay, thanks.'

'You need backup?' Nate asked. 'My father's got me running security for the blood drives. I'm bored,' he admitted.

'I've got back up, but I'll call you when the shit hits the fan,' I promised.

'See that you do.' Nate rang off.

We arrived at the Arrowe Park Hospital. It was a grey January day and everything looked dull and dismal. The clouds were full and I was glad I had my jacket.

We parked in the free carpark. As usual it was rammed, but I managed to find a space for my car that would do. That was one advantage of having my small run-around. I put a full body harness onto Gato to help lend him the air of a 'service dog', and we got out and headed to the main building. Tom knew the way, so we let him take the lead.

We were all in the Other realm. As we passed through the door into Ward 32A, we were stopped by a witch in a nurse's uniform. She had one triangle on her forehead. 'You need to sign in,' she said briskly. 'Who are you visiting?'

'Catriona Barnes.'

The nurse frowned. 'The wizard.' It wasn't a question.

Hes opened her mouth to correct her and I stood on her foot. 'That's right.' I'd forgotten that Hes hadn't got the memo that mermaids were kind of an open secret.

The nurse wrote down our names on a clipboard, and I did a quick scan of other visitors. Just above our names, Bastion Urvan was down as visiting Charlize. Bingo. Then I grimaced. The nurse dotted her i's with big hoops, like a child. It didn't inspire confidence in her abilities.

'Follow me,' the nurse said.

'I'm just going to pop to the loo,' I said. 'Something I ate hasn't agreed with me.' People don't tend to ask questions if you say that.

The nurse directed me to the toilet then the others followed her. Hes took Gato's lead. I wished I could get him to stay with me, but it would seem weird to take him with me.

I waited until they were out of sight then I started peeking in through the windows on the doors. Ogre. Troll. Cuthbert and Audrey with Emory. Oops! I ducked away from that door quickly. Emory wouldn't be thrilled at finding me tracking down Bastion alone. Better to ask for forgiveness after the event rather than permission before it.

A griffin lay in a bed in the room next to Audrey. There was a grim-faced man sitting next to her, facing the door. The whiteboard above the bed gave the patient's name as Charlize. I pushed open the door.

The man sitting beside the bed flicked his eyes towards me. He was tanned, with dark hair and dark eyes, and dressed in black combat trousers and a black hoodie. He was muscle bound and tense, like an off-duty soldier. His face showed nothing – I wouldn't have wanted to play poker with him – but there was a readiness about him that made me nervous, as if he could spring across the room in a second. He looked to be in his mid-thirties.

'Bastion?' I asked.

'Jessica Sharp,' he replied, without battling an eyelid.

Unnerved, I swallowed hard. 'You killed my parents.'

He raised an eyebrow. 'Did I?' he asked softly.

'Shirdal said it was your work,' I said as confidently as I could manage. My instincts were screaming at me to run away. I knew on some level that Bastion was an alpha predator. Everything in me wanted to flee except my stubborn nature and my need for justice. I wasn't going to run from my parents' killer.

'Shirdal isn't often wrong,' he conceded. *True.*

'Who hired you?'

'In which instance?'

My jaw clenched. 'Who hired you to kill my parents?'

'Ah. I have a confidentiality clause in all of my contracts that can only be waived by my employer.'

'You're going to break it,' I said firmly but hollowly. I had no idea how I was going to make him talk. Physically, he clearly had the edge.

The faintest smile touched his lips and I could see that he knew exactly what I was thinking. I had nothing here, no power, no bargaining chips. 'I brought you here for a reason,' he admitted.

I glared. 'I brought myself here.'

'Only because I let you. Or more accurately, your friend Mo.' A chill ran down my spine at the thought of what Bastion could do to Mo who had no idea about the deadly realm I'd involved him in.

'You leave him out of this,' I snapped.

Bastion ignored me and gestured to the griffin that lay prostrate in the bed. 'This is my daughter. I am an assassin, not a private investigator. Point me in the right direction and there is no one I can't kill. I know all the deadly arts, including poisoning. This illness is not natural, but it's not a poison I recognise.'

I nodded, waiting to see where he was going with this. I'd already decided this virus wasn't just a new bug; it was too selective, and it didn't seem to be contagious.

'You're an investigator. Find out who did this to my daughter and if it can be undone. Then I will tell you what you seek.'

'You will tell me who killed my parents?'

'I will tell you who hired me,' he confirmed.

I licked my lips. 'Okay. I'll find out who did this to Charlize, and you'll tell me who hired you to kill my parents.'

'It is agreed,' Bastion intoned.

I had a feeling that I'd literally made a deal with the devil. 'Why me? I'm sure there are other investigators out there you could hire, who know the ins and outs of the realms.'

'There are,' he conceded. 'But none of the others are truth seekers.'

I tried to keep my own poker face in place with limited success. 'Who said I was a truth seeker?'

'Your parents.'

Rage flared, sudden, wild and uncontrollable. Had he tortured them to get this information? As far as I knew they had never told anyone what I was, yet he knew. Their bodies had been so much flesh and bone when he was done with them that they'd had to be identified from their dental records.

With an inarticulate sound of rage I flew towards Bastion – but Nate stopped me before I reached him by phasing out of the shadows directly into my path. His eyes widened as he took in Bastion, who was still sitting in his chair and eyeing me like I was a fly he could swat whenever he chose. Nate's arms pinned mine to my side, and his solid body stopped me in my path.

'God damn it!' I snarled. I stopped myself before I could order Nate to let me go. I hadn't used my command bond with him, and I didn't intend to start now, no matter how much I wanted to.

Nate met my eyes, all hints of humour gone. 'Calm down, Jinx. Take a deep breath. If I let you go right now, you're going to get yourself killed by a griffin.'

I struggled in his arms, but vampyrs are ridiculously strong as well as fast.

Bastion interrupted the moment. 'Your parents told me that information voluntarily and without duress.' *True.*

What the hell? I stopped struggling and looked at him, genuinely bewildered. 'I don't understand.'

'You don't, but you will. You're tenacious. They said you were.'

I blinked and shook my head stupidly. I was so confused that my head was pounding.

'Send your friend on his way,' Bastion suggested, 'and we can continue our tête-à-tête.'

I focused on Nate. He was still wrapped around me, and he smelled nice and reassuring. His presence soothed me. 'I'm all right,' I said slowly. 'Give us some space.'

Nate let go of me and stepped back. 'You're sure?'

I sent him a mock glare. 'I said I'd call you when the shit hit the fan.'

He looked at me innocently. 'I was bored. Besides, when the shit hits the fan it's too late to call. I thought I'd come hang, just in case. I felt your anger and I came running.'

'A nice opportunity to look heroic in front of Hes?' I

suggested with a teasing smirk. He didn't deny it. 'I'm sorry she missed you saving the day.' My smile faded. 'Now get. Wait outside.' My controlling bond flared – I'd inadvertently given Nate an order. Goddamn it. He moved to the door seconds after the words left my mouth. 'Sorry!' I called. 'You can come back if you want.'

Nate grimaced but left the room anyway. I'd been so good at making sure I didn't order him around. Free will is a precious thing, not something I'd willingly take away from anyone. I glared at Bastion. 'You're making a real mess of my life.'

'You're doing that all on your own,' he stated.

'So I'm a truth seeker. Why do you want me on the case more than anyone else? Being a lie detector is handy, but it doesn't make up for a wealth of knowledge about the realms. Why choose me?'

His eyebrow rose. '*Because* you're a truth seeker. The clue is in the name. You can seek the truth.'

I rolled my eyes. 'Well, thank you, Captain Obvious.'

'Careful, Jessica,' he murmured, his eyes flinty and hard. Ah, yes: let's not make the deadly assassin mad. 'Why do you think truth seekers are so rare?' he asked. He continued before I could respond. 'It's because every time one was found, they were taken by the powers-that-be at the time, whatever or whoever they might be. They didn't get to mate and breed true like the rest of us. They were taken and used. In times gone by, the vampyrs were in charge or the wolves or the dragons. Now it's the Connection. Your power isn't just in being a lie detector, it's being a truth seeker. You can touch anyone and divine anything you want about them.'

I felt my jaw drop open. Suddenly I remembered telling Jack that his favourite colour was green when he'd been holding my hand. Son of a bitch. He had told me that there was no need for me to divine anything further; Jack knew more about my powers than I did. Hell, it seemed everyone did. My mind flashed to the vision I'd seen of Conrad. I'd touched him, wondered how he'd died and seen his last moments. My powers even worked on the newly dead.

My foundations were roiling under my feet and I felt vaguely nauseous. A further thought occurred to me. 'So I can divine any truth?' I asked. Bastion nodded. 'So I can touch you and find out who hired you to kill my parents?'

'Yes. And because I wouldn't be telling you, that will get around my confidentiality clause nicely.'

I started towards him, and he surprised me with a wry smile. 'Not now. After you've found who has orchestrated this mess. Then you can divine whatever you like.'

'What's to stop me now?' I asked belligerently.

His smile widened. 'Your conscience.'

I opened my mouth to say to hell with my conscience, but my upbringing – my whole being – disagreed. I'd made an agreement. Now that I had learnt that I could circumvent it, it didn't mean that I should. I was who I was because of my integrity. I frequently learnt things that I shouldn't; discretion and patience were parts of my toolset. Still I wrestled with myself. I was so close to getting answers.

Bastion watched me struggle with myself confidently, arrogantly. I really wanted to lunge across the room, touch him and force the secret out of his mind, but I didn't for two reasons. Firstly, I doubted I'd get two steps before he put me down, and secondly, that behaviour would make my parents ashamed of me. That put a lump in my throat and my conscience firmly back in control.

He read my decision on my face. From nowhere, he produced a business card. It had nothing on it but a telephone number, his own presumably. I pocketed it silently and cast around for a subject change. 'So why are you here?' I waved at the hospital surroundings.

'By my daughter's bedside? Is it so hard to imagine that I care about her?' His voice was mocking and full of self-loathing.

'Yes,' I said simply.

He smiled. 'It's been a long time since someone has dared to be rude to me. It's refreshing.' The smile vanished. 'And annoying.'

I swallowed hard again.

'My daughter is an assassin. She may be targeted

135

while she is in a weakened state. I am here to prevent such attempts.' *True.*

'Why have you brought her here if you're concerned for her safety?'

'I was persuaded against my better judgment. Shirdal and the Prime Elite thought it best that all victims receive the same medical care. It will give the medical staff the best opportunity to find a cure if they have access to all of the species at once. They can work out the common features of the illness.'

'And they wouldn't usually have such access?' I asked.

'No. Ward 34A is rarely used, but desperate times call for desperate measures.'

'What do you know?' I asked. 'Who did Charlize encounter recently?'

'She's an assassin,' Bastion said flatly. 'She is subject to the same confidentiality agreements as me.'

'So you don't know anything,' I summed up flatly. Some part of me knew it was a bad idea to piss off the scary assassin, but the other stupider part of me couldn't resist putting the boot in.

Bastion eyed me, his face immovable as granite. 'I don't know anything.'

'I'll have to dig into her activities.'

'If you must. It will be difficult, and you risk the anger of her employers.'

I nodded. He wasn't telling me anything I didn't

already know, but this was a high stakes game, and I wasn't going to pull out because it was a little scary.

I'd been putting it off, but now I knew more about my powers it was time to use them. I concentrated and stepped closer to Charlize. She was in griffin form. Her feathers looked dull and lifeless, and her wings were folded behind her. Her eyes were closed and her chest rose and fell shallowly. I closed my eyes and let the ocean recede. Despair rose in me, sharp and distinct. It wasn't coming from me or Charlize.

I opened my eyes. 'You'll have to step outside,' I said firmly, 'I can't get anything from her with your emotions rolling over me.' I wasn't sure if that was true, but he was certainly distracting me.

He raised an eyebrow. 'I will control my emotions.' Just like that, his despair was silenced, and I got absolutely nothing from him. He was one scary dude.

I closed my eyes and concentrated on the ocean once more, then I let it recede. Nothing. I stepped closer to Charlize and touched her feathered head.

How did you get sick?

She was in a crowd, focused on the target ahead of her. Something sharp was slipped into her flesh. She looked around. A kid was smiling apologetically. 'Sorry, lady, I tripped.' He was holding a badge with an open pin. She flicked her eyes back to her target who was rapidly disappearing. She took two steps forwards, and the world went sideways.

I gasped as I pulled back into myself. She'd been injected with something, I was sure of it. And I'd recognised her target.

It was Stone.

CHAPTER 13

T HE DOOR BANGED open and Emory ran in, his jaw tight, emerald eyes blazing. His hands were held in front of him, and fire was sizzling on his fingertips. Yeesh.

Nate followed. He met my eyes and looked vaguely apologetic. Emory must have spotted him loitering outside the room and figured out where I was. It looked like Emory had panicked when he'd heard I was in a room with the deadliest assassin that ever lived. It would have been quite touching if he hadn't looked so angry.

'Prime Elite.' Bastion greeted Emory casually with an inclination of his head, ignoring the fire that licked at Emory's hands. Then he turned his attention back to me. Obviously he didn't see Emory as a threat, which was either brave or foolish. 'Anything?' Bastion asked me.

'Something,' I confirmed.

Emory's nostrils flared, and he glared at me. 'I told you to stay away from Bastion.' His tone was flat. He was still tense, but he let the fire extinguish as he took in the relative calm of the room.

'You did,' I agreed. 'But you're my boyfriend, not my boss.'

'Currently I am both,' Emory said tightly. 'I hired you to look into the virus.'

'So did Bastion. I'm not quite sure what you're having a fit over.'

'He's not happy about our meeting, Jessica Sharp,' Bastion said, as if I really didn't know what the issue was.

'Yes, thank you, Bastion. I'd gathered that.'

'It's almost like the Prime Elite doesn't trust me.' Bastion spoke quietly, but there was nothing soft about his tone. 'You ordered me not to harm her, Prime, and I have not done so.'

Emory ordered him not to harm me? What the hell was going on here? I knew there was more to the Prime title than I'd thought, but why was Bastion obeying Emory?

'I ordered you not to meet with her,' Emory snarled. 'Yet here you are.'

Bastion nodded and gave a small smile, but his eyes stayed flat and dead. 'She found me.' He said it innocently, like he hadn't baited the trap that I'd sprung.

'Enough bickering,' I intervened firmly. 'Bastion and I have agreed to work towards a common goal. No one is killing anyone just now.'

'How dull,' Nate commented. 'Nothing like the joke.'

I took the bait. 'What joke?'

Bastion answered for him. 'A dragon, a vampyr and a griffin walked into a bar.'

I waited a beat. 'And?' I asked. 'What's the punchline?'

'Nothing. They all killed each other.' Bastion shrugged.

Nate snickered. 'The old ones are the good ones.'

I sighed. 'Not all species are evil, you know. There is good and bad in everything. You can't just decide that a whole species deserve death. It's ludicrous.'

Nate flashed Emory a grin. 'Next thing, she's going to suggest me as your best man.'

I flushed bright red. 'We're not quite at the marriage stage yet, thank you.'

Nate raised an eyebrow. 'You may not be, but he ran in here like his mate was in danger.'

'Thank you, Nathaniel,' Emory glared.

'Well,' I said faux enthusiastically, 'this has been fun. But I'm supposed to be in another room right now, so I'll leave you to it.'

Emory shook his head. 'I'll come with you. I need to speak to Jack.'

Nate said nothing; he just walked into the shadows and disappeared.

Bastion steepled his fingers and watched silently. I gave him a finger wave. 'Ciao.' He watched me impassively. Tough crowd.

Emory and I walked out of the room. I was intent on finding Catriona, but Emory had other ideas. He pulled me into a supplies closet. 'This isn't your most romantic date,' I said lightly.

He let out a noise best described as a growl and leaned down to kiss me. The kiss was hard and bruising, and it only took me a moment to get on board. His hands were on my waist, lifting me up easily. I wrapped my legs around him and let him carry me as if I were feather light.

Light flooded in. 'This isn't a hotel,' a disapproving voice said. 'Get a room. A hotel room. Not a supplies room. Out!'

Somewhat sheepishly, I let my legs drop and kept my face averted as we sidled out. I didn't want to look that particular nurse in the face. Emory laced his fingers with mine and kept his head up. He wasn't embarrassed at all. He tugged me to a stop in front of Catriona's door. 'We're not done here,' he said slowly. 'We have things to discuss.'

'Sure. Okey-dokey.'

A smile pulled at his lips despite himself, and he shook his head. If I'd had to guess what he was thinking, it would be that I was a total dweeb.

He knocked once on the door jamb, and we walked into the room. Jack was sitting next to Catriona's bed, and Gato was resting his head by her feet. Hes and Tom were leaning against the wall opposite. 'Howdy,' I said to the room at large.

'That's some tummy trouble you have there,' Jack teased, looking at Emory's hand joined with mine and my lips puffy from kissing.

'Yup,' I agreed. 'I must have eaten something bad.'

'I hate it when that happens.' Jack turned back to Catriona. 'You'll like Catriona. She's fun. She has a good sense of humour, too.'

'There's a bit of an age gap between you.'

'She's a friend,' he said defensively.

'Who you're in love with,' I pointed out.

He didn't deny it. 'We grew up together – she's my youngest sister's best friend. At some point she turned my head, but we agreed we'd wait until after she'd had her shore leave.'

'You two agreed or you suggested?'

Jack ran his hand through his long green hair. 'I suggested,' he conceded. 'She needed to do some living first, then I'd know that she really wanted me.'

'You sent her out hoping she'd come back,' I stated.

'Yes,' he said tightly, looking at her prostrate form. 'More fool me.'

'Who did you send her with? There was a purse of them on shore leave, right?'

'Yeah, there were four of them together. Two of them returned a month ago. They'd split up from Catriona and Emma a while ago.'

'And where is Emma?'

He shook his head. 'I don't know.'

I sighed. 'And you didn't think to mention this earlier because…?'

Jack shook his head. 'The two who returned said Catriona and Emma had a falling out. I didn't think it was relevant.'

'Get your people on it,' I said firmly. 'See if anyone can reach Emma.'

Jack pulled out his phone as I looked around the crowded room. No way was I going to feel anything from Catriona among this crowd. 'Everyone out,' I commanded. 'Except for Gato. He can watch my back.' To my surprise, Emory moved to the door and gestured for Tom to follow. I'd expected some kind of token protest from him but I was glad when it didn't come.

Once Gato and I were alone with Catriona, I closed my eyes and focused on the ocean. I let its sounds wash over me and gradually recede. I felt love, all-consuming, pervasive love. Its strength made my heart ache.

I opened my eyes and saw Gato. He touched his snout to my hand and gave it a lick. My eyes welled up. 'I love you too, boy.' I kissed his head. 'I'm so grateful for you,' I murmured. He snuggled into me, and I let myself enjoy the feeling of love and protection. He would protect me from anyone, no matter the cost. 'Back at you,' I whispered, then swallowed past the lump in my throat.

'Come on. We're not here to snuggle.'

I drew back from him and walked closer to Catriona. Gato kept his distance at the other side of the room so I could concentrate. I wasn't getting anything from her. I needed to know how she'd fallen sick. I touched her forehead.

She was working. She sent a flirtatious smile to the sexy man who was standing alone, propping up the bar. He looked lonely; she'd be happy to chat to him to take his mind off his troubles. But first she had to deal with a group of lads nearby who were getting rowdier by the second. The new girl was sending panic signals so she moseyed over and made a few harmless remarks to take their attention off the newbie.

Someone knocked into her and she felt a sharp scratch on her arm. 'What the hell?' she yelled, turning to see which prick had hurt her. She kept turning. Someone poured a drink on her and she smelled vodka. 'She's drunk,' she heard someone say. Then they lifted her up by her armpits and she lost consciousness.

My mouth was dry. It couldn't be a coincidence. The lone man at the bar … it was Stone. I didn't know what was going on, but he was neck deep in it.

CHAPTER 14

I COULD FIND out how Catriona had got sick and was kidnapped, but I didn't know who had done it. Things weren't looking good for Stone right now, but I wondered if I could divine more. I needed to know who'd taken her.

I touched Catriona's hand lightly again and went deeper.

I felt sick. I hurt. It was an effort to raise my head, but I was being ordered to. I was in the water, floating, floating. A voice came out of nowhere. 'Give me some scales, Catriona. Give them freely. Do it, now.' He whistled and the tune compelled me. I obeyed sluggishly.

I flicked my tail out of the water, spraying the man with the discarded scales. They shone as they left me, leaving patches of my skin bare and aching. My brain wasn't working right; I was muzzy headed and lost.

Beyond my captor was another tank, and Emma was in it. My heart started to race as I registered her bare tail and her complete stillness. She had been de-scaled. Gods, was she dead?

The fear cleared my mind, and I looked around in

panic.

My strawberry-blond captor smiled at me. If the fear hadn't been all-pervading, I might have thought him handsome. 'None of that, Catriona. Sleep.' He whistled a tune and sleep came and dragged me down, kicking and screaming.

I gasped as I returned to myself. Gato was licking my face and whining slightly. I'd gone too deeply into Catriona, and for a moment I'd been her. My heart was still racing with the vestiges of her panic, her fear. I guess we knew now what had happened to poor Emma.

Catriona didn't know who her captor was but I did. There was no mistaking Ronan Fallows, one of the two people that I had killed in this life. So how had Catriona escaped, and why had she turned up now? We needed to know more about Ronan's lab – but now I wasn't sure that Stone was the right person to ask.

Gato licked me again. 'I'm okay,' I reassured him. 'I think I went too deep for a minute.' I shook off my confusion and called everyone back in. Emory, Tom, Nate, Hes and Jack were joined by Shirdal but no one seemed bothered by his presence. The room was packed.

Emory tilted his head, indicating that I should give the rundown.

I met Jack's eyes sympathetically. 'She was kidnapped,' I confirmed. 'She was held against her will. Ronan was in this up to his eyeballs. He piped her and made her give her scales willingly.'

Jack's jaw tightened, and he clenched his fists. 'Our scales have magical properties, but only if they are given freely.'

'Emma was with her.' I shook my head. 'Catriona didn't know for sure … but she thought Emma might be dead.'

'If Ronan wasn't already dead, I'd kill him again,' Jack snarled.

'Steady,' Emory cautioned. 'We need level heads.'

'Easy for you to say when the woman you love is absolutely fine!' Jack gestured at me.

Emory's eyes flashed and his nostrils flared. Tom tensed next to him, and the tension in the room shot up. Instinctively I stepped closer to Jack and touched his arm. 'We're going to save her,' I promised and was relieved when it buzzed *true*. Deep down, I believed that we could.

Jack opened his mouth and closed it with a clack. His eyes welled with tears and I felt his impotence. He could do nothing; he didn't know how to fight an enemy he couldn't see, and he needed direction. I squeezed his arm. 'We need to track Emma's movements,' I said. 'Maybe then we can pinpoint some locations or people all the victims have seen.'

Jack stood up stiffly. As he started to walk out, he paused next to Emory. 'Forgive me, my Prime. No disrespect was intended. I am not myself.'

Emory inclined his head in acknowledgement and the tension dissipated.

'We need to find out the location of the lab,' I said firmly. Tom and Shirdal nodded and ducked out of the room. 'Hes, you and Nate see if you can track down Emma's movements. You have access to the search programs that Jack doesn't – I just wanted to keep him busy.'

Hes nodded, her expression serious. For once, her face showed her emotions instead of the blank mask she had taken to wearing when she was around Nate. She was eager to prove herself. 'We can take my car,' Nate offered. As the two made their way out, I felt a glimmer of hope. It wasn't mine; it was coming from him.

Emory and I were left alone in Catriona's room. 'I should see if I can work out how Audrey and Cuthbert got sick,' I suggested.

Emory agreed and we went into their room. When I touched Audrey, her vision was short but it followed the same pattern. She was shopping in town with Cuthbert when they were swept into a crowd. Suddenly Audrey had felt a sting in her arm. She saw a young boy who held out a badge as an explanation and apologised with a grin. She swayed, but Cuthbert had reached out and steadied her. His touch had strengthened her, rejuvenated her, and they'd walked on, unaware of what had happened. Watching the vision now, I saw the young boy frown after them.

I told Emory what I had seen. 'We need to see who that boy is,' he said. 'We'll get a witch to scry it from your mind.'

I didn't like the thought of a witch scrambling around in my brain. 'Amber DeLea?' I suggested. She wasn't local but I had met her several times and I trusted her avarice, if nothing else. Besides, I'd rather not have a complete stranger crawling through my thoughts.

Emory took out his phone and made a call. 'Get Amber DeLea here,' he ordered then hung up.

'Lousy phone manners,' I commented again. It didn't even get me a smirk. Emory wasn't happy.

He kissed Audrey and Cuthbert on their foreheads. 'I'll be back as soon as I can,' he promised as he opened the door. Four brawny-looking men dressed in black were loitering outside. 'Two inside, two outside at all times,' Emory barked. 'Rotate in four-hour shifts. I don't want anyone tired.' The men nodded and assumed their posts.

We left the hospital in silence, Gato trotting happily at our heels. When we reached my small car, Emory grimaced but didn't complain. I drove us home in an uncomfortable silence.

I made us a brew and let Gato into the garden to pee. 'Give us a few minutes,' I said to him softly. He wagged his agreement and went upstairs to give us some privacy – and curled up on my bed, no doubt.

I handed Emory his tea and waited for what I knew was coming. He didn't leave me waiting long. 'He's an assassin! Jinx, he is *the* assassin. You piss him off, and he'll kill you. For all his words, I can't truly control him. He's outside the rules of polite society. What were you thinking?' His voice rose steadily in volume.

'I was thinking that he killed my parents and nothing – not you nor him – will stop me finding the mastermind behind their deaths.' My voice rose to meet his and I looked at him angrily. Nothing would stop me finding out who'd killed them. Some part of me accepted that although Bastion may have dealt the blow, he was nothing more than a gun or a knife; he was the weapon, not the instigator. I wanted to find who was responsible. I *needed* to. That had been my sole focus for years and I wasn't going to let anyone tell me otherwise, not even Emory.

He read the stubbornness in the line of my jaw. He ran a hand through his hair and sighed, his anger falling away as swiftly as it had risen. 'I don't want to stop you, I just want you safe.' *True.*

'This means everything to me,' I said finally. 'I won't ever be content until I know the truth. My parents' deaths haunt me. They are there all the time, niggling at me. And I'm closer than I've ever been. Now I know that I can seek the truth, it's within my reach.'

Emory blew out a breath. 'You need to be careful how you use your powers. If you seek the truth in the wrong person, they'll tell the realms what you are and every faction will want a piece of you. If you seek the truth, you need to be prepared to clear their minds afterwards. And I know how you feel about that.'

I grimaced. I didn't like it, but everything he said was true. 'I'll be careful, and I'll do what's necessary.'

The tension leached out of him. 'That's all that I ask.' He stepped closer. 'Was this our first fight? It wasn't so bad.'

'Guess it's time to kiss and make up,' I suggested.

'I like the way you think.' He pulled me into his arms and kissed me passionately. I moaned into his mouth. I needed *more*. I pushed his suit jacket from his shoulders and it fell to the floor. I unbuttoned his black shirt until I'd revealed the firm planes of his stomach. My hands skirted over him, enjoying the feel of his hard body against mine. My fingers drifted to his belt – and then his hands stilled mine. He pulled back. He was breathing heavily and his eyes were dark. 'We'd best stop there.' His voice was low and gravelly.

I blinked. Before I could reconnect my mouth to my brain I asked, 'What's wrong? Why are we always stopping? Don't you want me?'

He pulled me to him and crushed his mouth to mine. This time it was his hands that wandered. He pushed me back into a chair and the space between us sizzled. He groaned and slid to his knees between my legs. He looked up at me, his chest pulling in heavy lungfuls of air. 'God, I want you Jess. And if we'd just fucked in that limo, things would have been simpler.'

'What? Why?' I wasn't at my most articulate.

'Because I didn't love you then,' he continued, as if he hadn't just dropped a bombshell. 'When a dragon is in love and has sex, it's the start of the mating bond. It's the betrothal. When we have sex, it's with a promise that you'll be mine forever.'

My mouth was dry. He was so confident that I was his mate. 'No take-backsies?' I asked lightly, because the conversation was too serious, too heavy and altogether terrifying.

Emory's eyes warmed. 'No take-backsies,' he confirmed.

'I might not be your mate,' I suggested.

'You are.' *True.*

'You believe I am, but I might not be. You just ... fixated on me at an early age because of the whole rescuing thing,' I said uncomfortably. 'Like a baby duck, you know? You imprinted on me.'

'Like a duck.' He spoke slowly.

I nodded. His eyes glittered dangerously; he didn't like the duck thing. 'Maybe like a peacock?' I said hastily, thinking of their plumage.

'Pea. Cock.' He repeated it slowly, like I was insulting his male appendage.

Oh hell, I was making things worse. 'I'm not calling your—' I stopped abruptly. 'It felt magnificent through your trousers. I wasn't saying... I'm just saying, you know. Like a duck.'

'Like a duck,' he repeated flatly.

'You met me when you were so young, Emory, so vulnerable, and I rescued you. Hero worship is normal in those circumstances, but I'm no hero. You need to be sure. When it walks like a duck, talks like a duck...'

His eyes were unfriendly. 'This is not what I envisaged would happen the first time I told a woman I loved her,' he muttered.

I instantly felt guilty. Here he was, pouring out his heart, and here I was casting doubts on his feelings. He was an adult, a two-hundred-year-old one at that; he was old enough to know his own mind. Just because I didn't know mine, it was no reason to cast aspersions on his.

'I'm sorry,' I said softly. 'I have all these abandonment issues and it makes it hard to let you in. I like you a whole lot. I lust after you more than it's decent to admit. But love is a scary one for me in lots of ways. I don't know my own heart, but I—' I paused. 'Thank you for loving me.'

Emory shook his head in disbelief but he smiled. 'Both human and dragon women throw themselves at me, yet the woman that I love thinks I'm a duck.'

'I don't think you're an *actual* duck,' I protested.

'I'm a dragon,' Emory purred, eyes flashing. 'Perhaps it's time I showed you one of my skills.' He reached up to my trousers and unfastened the button, giving me plenty of time to protest. I wasn't sure quite what he was proposing, given that he'd just said we couldn't have sex without becoming permanently … engaged.

I lifted my hips up and he slid my trousers and knickers down in one go. He started to kiss his way up the inside of my legs. 'Dragons,' he explained, 'have excellent tongue stamina.' He flashed me a predatory smile.

Oh boy!

CHAPTER 15

MY HEART WAS still pounding. Emory was looking smug. He wasn't wrong; he had put his tongue to excellent use. Three times. I lifted an impossibly heavy hand to reach for him, to reciprocate but he shook his head. 'Not now,' he said gently. 'Not until you know how you feel about me. I'll go and have a shower. When I'm downstairs, we should discuss our strategy.'

I felt boneless and content. 'Strategy,' I agreed.

He grinned, all smug male pride that he could reduce my brain to mush, then gave me a quick kiss and pushed off to borrow my shower.

Eventually I got my limbs working again and went into the kitchen to make us some sandwiches, enough for a small army. When Emory came down, his hair was wet but he was as immaculate as ever in his ridiculously expensive suit. 'Jeans are comfier than suits,' I pointed out.

'I'm expected to convey a certain image. Jeans don't really fit the profile.'

He wolfed down several sandwiches with a coffee. It

was gone 2 p.m., so we still had plenty of the day to work with.

'I called Stone on the way to the hospital and asked him about the lab,' I explained. 'He said he'd do some digging. That was before the ... visions that showed he was involved. So now I'm thinking that wasn't my smartest move. But still, a part of me still believes he's innocent. He's a soldier of the Connection, but he has a strong moral compass. He wouldn't do something he didn't think was right.' That was true. But Stone's definition of right and wrong might be different to mine.

Emory grimaced.

'I know you don't like him,' I said, 'but the fact that I exchanged saliva with him doesn't change the fact that he is a good man.' Mostly, except the whole compelling-me-to-trust-him thing, but I didn't think reminding Emory of that was a good idea.

'Don't remind me,' Emory muttered. 'I'm struggling not to get all territorial right now.'

I narrowed my eyes at him. 'If you pee on me to mark your territory, that is not okay.'

He flashed me a grin. 'No golden showers. Check.'

I blushed bright red. 'Well, unless it's something you like,' I stuttered. 'I mean, never say never.'

His grin widened. 'It's not something that floats my boat, but I'm pleased to hear you're open to new experiences.'

'I'm twenty-five, not two hundred, so there are still a fair few new experiences in front of me. And erm—' man, this was uncomfortable '—I haven't been with that many guys. Just so you know.'

Emory got up from the dining room table and pulled me into a hug. He kissed my forehead. 'I'm not in a hurry. We've got plenty of time to explore things between us.'

He smelled good. How did he still smell so good even when he used my shower gel? Something about his scent was underlyingly masculine. I cleared my throat. 'We're good?'

'We're good,' Emory confirmed. 'But we're not calling Stone.' He pulled out his phone and dialled Ajay Ven. He put it on speaker and held the phone between us.

'Prime, how can I help you?' Ajay's tone was respectful, almost deferential, not the jokey cavalier tone he used with me.

'Are you free to talk?' Emory asked brusquely.

'The line is secure,' Ajay confirmed.

'I'm with Jinx. She can hear you too.'

'Hi Jinx, how are you going?' That sounded like the Ajay I knew.

'I'm okay. We're digging into these illnesses. It's pretty clear the victims have all been injected with something, and we need to find out what. Ronan and his lab are looking like the main suspects.'

'The lab was closed down over a month ago,' Ajay countered.

'Even so, Ronan was involved. What are the chances that his lab was cooking something other than drugs? I'm all but certain he was making a virus. If nothing else, he was involved in collecting ingredients. Luckily it seems the virus needs to be injected rather than simply being airborne, but I'd say the illnesses we've seen so far have been trials before someone decides to make it widespread. We need to get the jump on this. The only reason we've got as far as we have is because the creatures are talking to each other.'

'They wouldn't expect that,' Ajay mused. 'The creatures are supposed to keep themselves to themselves.'

'It was deemed safer to portray it that way when the human races started joining us in the Other,' Emory explained for my benefit rather than Ajay's.

'So we've started to connect the dots sooner than they'd like,' I said. 'That might make them move their timetable up. We need to find the lab.'

'There's a problem with that,' Ajay warned. 'There's been a spate of fires lately, an unusual number of them. The first was Ronan's lab. It was destroyed.'

'Damn it.' I sighed. 'Do you know it's location?'

'It was in Wales, near Bala Lake.'

Alarm bells rang. The troll compound I'd been to was located near Bala, and they'd been having a dispute with the mermaids because something was polluting the lake. Maybe it wasn't accidental pollution; maybe it had been deliberate.

'Text me the location,' Emory ordered.

'Yes, Prime,' Ajay responded instantly.

'Text us the locations of the other fires as well,' I suggested.

'Will do.'

After we rang off, I raised an eyebrow at Emory. 'All right, so what's Ajay's deal?'

He didn't pretend to misunderstand me. 'He's brethren. He's one of my spies in the Connection.'

I blinked. 'I thought you were his informant.'

'The other way around,' Emory said easily.

'You have spies,' I stated flatly.

'Of course. Only a fool would ignore an organisation as big as the Connection. I might not belong to it, or agree with it, but I can't pretend it doesn't exist. It's a significant threat to all creature kind.'

I let that sink in. There was definitely more to the Prime title than I knew if Emory was building a network of spies. Surely the king of the dragons, a small group of supernatural shifters, didn't need to go to such lengths.

'You still haven't introduced me to any other dragons,' I said in a non-sequitur.

'You've met Audrey and Cuthbert,' he countered. 'They're closer to me than anyone in my court.'

'Yes, but you *have* a court and you've kept it from me. Why?'

He studied me. 'Until we're mated, you'd be vulnerable there. There are factions that seek to undermine me, and harming you would be the surest way to do it. It would show that I'm too weak to protect you. I'm keeping you to myself to keep you safe.'

'And?' I asked. I could hear there was more.

'And ... I don't want my court to scare you away.'

'I'm pretty robust,' I said. 'I don't scare easily.'

He ran his hand through his hair. 'I have to be different in my court. Firmer. I'm not sure you'd like that Emory.'

'You can't just keep a part of you locked away. I can handle a tough-guy routine.'

'And if it's not a routine?'

'Then I need to know that, too. I can't ... mate ... with you only knowing half the story. At a certain point, you're going to have to trust me.'

Emory looked at me honestly. 'I do trust you, and if you loved me maybe I could take that step. But you're not sure of me yet, not sure of *us*. I'm not going to risk destroying this before it's even started.'

I understood but that didn't mean I liked it. I needed to know him, warts and all. 'When Stone and I were ... whatever ... he beheaded a vampyr in front of me. He was clearly waiting for me to freak out, and I didn't. I get that this is a different realm with different rules. Don't put obstacles in our path that might not be there.'

Emory's gaze was dark. Finally he sighed. 'Fine. When this is all over, I'll introduce you to my court.'

I reached over and took his hand. 'If you want me to be all in, I need that to happen. Knowledge dispels fear. I need to know you – all of you – before we can take the next step together.'

He took my hand and drew it to his lips. 'This is the most affection I'd be able to show you in my court.'

I wrapped my arms around his neck and pulled him closer. 'We'd better make use of all of this privacy then,' I said wickedly.

He grinned. 'I like the way you think.' That was the last we spoke for a good few minutes until Ajay's text disturbed the moment. 'We've got a location,' Emory said regretfully. 'We'd better get on the road.'

I put the details into Google maps, and I also texted the location to my friend Mo and asked him if he could find the legal owner of the property. I could do a land registry search, but I'd just turn up a shell company. I wanted Mo to dig into the owner behind the façade. I got an affirmative in response: Mo was on it.

I whistled to Gato, and he thundered down the stairs. 'Road trip,' I told him. 'We're going to Wales.' He took a big drink of water and wagged at me. He was good to go, and so was I. The quicker we cracked this, the better chance the victims had of surviving. And the sooner Bastion would answer my questions about my parents.

I chucked some spare clothes into a duffel as well as my usual supplies – lockpicks, disposable gloves and a flip blade. I grabbed some food for Gato and a sleeping bag for me, just in case, then I opened the front door. On my drive was a shiny black Mercedes G Wagon AMG, the same one I'd driven before.

Emory ducked down and pulled out the car keys that had been duct-taped to the underside of the car. He chucked them to me. 'Happy Christmas,' he grinned. 'Sorry it's late.'

I blew out a breath. To me, a car seemed like an extravagant gift, but Emory lived in a different world, and I'd helped get him there. I opened the door, and we all piled in. I turned to Emory. 'Thank you for the car,' I said finally. 'It seems like too much but I'm not going to be churlish, I'm just going to say thank you.' Mum taught me my manners.

He slid me a sideways glance. 'Get used to it, Jess. I have lots of money, and I like giving you things. It's fun to watch you squirm.'

I stuck out my tongue at him.

'Sexy,' he commented.

I ignored him and started the engine. I turned on the radio, and the Mercedes' tyres ran down the miles in no time at all. It was 4 p.m. when we arrived at the location that Ajay had given us. Night was starting to fall, and it seemed like the perfect time for some breaking and entering. It had been a while since my last retrieval op, and I'd missed the thrill.

We parked outside a large building that looked at odds with the area. It was built of concrete, and evidence of the fire was clear. The material might be resistant to flames and heat, but tale of the inferno was written all over it in blackened and spalled walls. There were massive cracks, and despite it being a one-storey building, it didn't look particularly safe.

There were no external security cameras, no safe-guarded perimeter. Whoever had run this facility was long gone. We got out of the car and made our way to the front doors. There was tape across the entrance put there by the police or the firefighters. I pulled on some disposable gloves and handed a set to Emory, then we slipped under it.

Night was approaching, and the building was already dark. Emory effortlessly created a few fire orbs, which he chucked above each of us to light our way.

The building was eerie and empty. The concrete walls and tiled floors did nothing to dampen the echo of our footfalls, and Gato's nails clicked as he walked. We ducked our heads into a couple of side rooms, but they were empty, devoid of furniture. They were dark and dank rooms, reminding me of cells. If the rest of this property was the same, we'd come all this way for nothing.

We reached a large room that still had a few metal desks that had survived the flames, though they were burnished and marked. On opposing walls were two empty metal tanks. We'd found where Emma and Catriona had been held. The windows were narrow and their glass had been destroyed. Cool air whistled into the laboratory, creating a ghostly howl.

I closed my eyes, tried to block out the noise, and concentrated on letting the ocean recede. I'd read an empty room before, so maybe I could do it now. As the ocean silenced, the hairs on my neck stood on end. I could feel despair so thick it made my eyes well up. Emma's, I thought. It chilled me.

I opened my eyes and concentrated on silencing the call of the ocean as I walked around the room. I touched the metal desk and was immediately transported to another moment.

'Burn it, Franklin,' a tall dark man ordered. 'Destroy it all.'

The other man, young, gangly and freckled, nodded. 'Yes, Sir Benedict.' He raised his hands and fire exploded outward. The dead mermaid's body crackled as it burned, and the young man felt sick.

I felt sick too. Suddenly I felt trapped, suffocating in a vision that I couldn't get out of. The vision started again, and my panic increased.

I *was* trapped.

CHAPTER 16

THE VISION STARTED again, though this time I didn't feel sick. I felt love – pervading, overwhelming love. Slowly I came back to myself, disorientated and confused. Emory was hugging me and stroking my hair, and Gato was pressed against my body whining. They were both looking at me with concern.

Emory let out a sharp breath of relief. 'Thank God you're back. You zoned out like you were in a trance. You couldn't hear me, and I couldn't reach you.' I could hear his panic.

'I'm okay,' I managed. *Lie.* I grimaced. I needed to get a handle on this; it seemed like I could get nothing at all or I went all in. Audrey really hadn't given me enough direction. With a start of guilt, I remembered the book she'd given me that I'd barely touched. I needed to find time for it; flipping through it wasn't safe.

'You saw something?' Emory asked.

I relayed the vision, just the one loop of it. He frowned. 'Empaths are only supposed to work on organic things – people, plants, living beings. How is it you can feel the echoes like this?'

I realised that I hadn't explained yet about Faltease and Glimmer making my parents Other, and about me being born of two created Others. I was something new and unique, and I didn't want to be. I wanted to be normal.

'Another time,' I said, instead of expressing all the thoughts I wanted to. 'We've got company.' The ocean was still silent, and I could feel someone coming; they were nervous and steeling themselves for something unpleasant. I got the feeling that the something unpleasant was us. I let the ocean return so I could focus, and I gathered my intention – but for what?

Gato let out a low growl and grew into his battle-cat form. He stalked forwards next to me. Emory turned and moved nearer to the entrance. We all waited, braced for an attack.

When it came, the attack was from behind. Flames shot in from the open windows, coming directly at me. Before I could do anything, Emory leapt into the shadows and emerged in front of me, moving with incredible speed. He threw himself in front of the flames, wrapping his arms around me and shielding me with his body.

'Emory!' I screamed in panic. I could see his suit burning, and I could feel the broiling heat. Fear and panic raced through me, disabling me. God, he couldn't survive this. Surely he couldn't survive this?

Gato ducked safely under the nearby metal table and waited out the flames. Finally, the flames died down, and I frantically turned Emory over, braced to see the most awful injuries. His suit jacket and shirt were burnt away from his back, but his skin was blessedly unmarked. 'What?' I said dumbly. 'How?'

He kissed me quickly. 'Dragon, impervious to fire,' he explained. 'I'm going after him. Stay here.' Before I could argue, he ran into the shadows again and disappeared. He was getting the hang of this phasing thing.

My heart was still racing – I'd thought that Emory was a goner for sure. I took several steadying breaths and tried to put my feelings in a box for later because I couldn't face them right now.

'Stay here,' I muttered eventually to Gato. 'Who does he think he is? King of everyone?' *True.* That made me blink. Shit, my subconscious believed that was true. I pulled the thought up and dusted it off. Emory might not be king of everyone, but he was definitely king of more than just the dragons. Something slotted into place.

'Prime Elite,' I said aloud. 'He's the king of all of the creatures, isn't he? Not just the dragons.' I didn't really expect a response from Gato, but it was undeniable that he nodded. My jaw dropped. 'Christ, is he king of you, too?' Gato shook his head side to side in a universal 'maybe' signal.

I remembered Jack kneeling to him, and Shirdal and

Bastion deferring to him. Yeah, Emory was king of more than just the dragons. And I was equally sure that it wasn't something the Connection knew about. Stone wouldn't have spoken to him the way he had if he'd known. Nate hadn't mentioned it, and I'm sure he would have done if he'd known, so it wasn't something the human side knew about. God, this realm was secrets wrapped in mysteries hidden in enigmas. It was a wonder anyone knew which way was up.

And where was I in all of this? I was a wizard, technically on the human side, but I was dating a dragon. The king of the dragons, of the creatures. If we mated, what the hell would that make me? Queen? And queen of what exactly?

I'm a lot of things, but royal isn't one of them. I pushed my head between my knees. I didn't want to be a queen, not of anyone. But man, I really liked Emory. When he'd flung himself in front of me like that, I'd thought he was going to die. In that moment I'd panicked so deeply that it shook me to my core. My only thought had been that I hadn't told him that I loved him. Fuck.

I don't know how long I was freaking out for before Emory returned, phasing out of the shadows, dragging a somewhat beaten-up elemental behind him.

Emory raised an eyebrow, and I straightened and pasted on a calm expression. Not freaking out at all. Nope, no siree, nothing to see here. I definitely wasn't hyperventilating while he was gone.

'Franklin,' I greeted the elemental from my recurring vision. 'How nice to meet you.'

Franklin was shaking visibly. 'How do you know my name?'

'A little birdie told me,' I said lightly. 'We've been looking for you, Franklin.' *Lie.* 'How kind of you to waltz in like this and save us all that trouble. So considerate.'

He was young, twenty at the most, and his eyes were wide with fear. 'What are you going to do to me?'

'I haven't decided,' I said honestly. 'You did try to roast me and my boyfriend, and that kind of thing is very much frowned on.'

'I didn't have a choice!' he cried. 'Benedict said if I didn't do it, he'd cast the living flare on me!' *True.*

I kept my face poker straight. I had no idea what a living flare was, but context suggested it wasn't a warm hug with kittens. 'We all have choices,' I said. 'You burnt the mermaid.'

'She was already dead. I haven't harmed anyone, I swear. I've just burnt up the places Benedict told me to.'

'Talk me through all of the targets.' I spoke flatly, like I knew all about them anyway.

'The lab was the first, then the trolls' bar. Then it was the ogres' boxing gym. Then it was the dryads' garden centre. I made sure to do it at night when they were empty,' Franklin said earnestly. 'Next was the gnomes' ironworks centre.'

Emory's face was like thunder and his arm tightened around Franklin's throat. Franklin let out a panicked squeak and looked at me in desperation. I was having a hard time working up any sympathy for him; he had wilfully destroyed people's homes and livelihoods. Yes, he did it under duress, and that cut him some slack, but he still deserved a few moments of terror.

I let him ride it out before I relented. 'You've made your point,' I said to Emory. 'Relax your hold on him.'

'You'll let me go?' Franklin asked hopefully.

I snorted. 'So you can run straight back to Benedict? No, I don't think so, Frankie. Sorry, but you're going to be detained – one way or another.' Detained sounded so much better than kidnapped. 'Do you know why Benedict had you start these fires?'

Franklin shook his head. 'I don't. I'm sorry. I'd tell you if I could.' *True.*

'Do you know who ordered the fires?'

'Benedict.' He looked confused.

'But who ordered Benedict?' I asked.

He shook his head. 'No one orders Benedict. Every-one obeys him and hopes he doesn't pick you for his next flare party.'

The word 'party' made it sound like a celebration. I got the feeling it was anything but. 'How did you know to come here now?' I queried.

'Benedict had a motion camera installed in case any-one came back. I was deployed when you arrived.'

I frowned. 'How?'

'How what?'

'How did you get here so fast?'

He looked confused. 'It took me about forty minutes to get here.'

It had taken us almost an hour. Somehow Benedict had been tipped off that we were on our way – and the only ones who could have tipped him off were Stone, or Ajay. I met Emory's hard gaze. He'd reached the same conclusion, and he wasn't happy about it.

Emory nodded at Franklin. 'Do you have any more questions for him, Jinx?'

'Do you know anything about a virus?' I asked.

Franklin shook his head. 'No,' he stuttered. *Lie.* 'I don't know anything.'

'Now why would you lie to me, Franklin?'

His face went beet red. 'I – I – please, he'll kill me if he knows I have them.'

'Have what?'

'I – took some notes from the lab before it burnt down. I thought they might be some security for me.'

Maybe Franklin wasn't quite as stupid as he seemed. 'Where are the papers now?' I asked.

'My flat.' Franklin's shoulders slumped. *True.*

I couldn't think of anything else that I needed to

know, and Franklin was depressing me. 'I'm done,' I said to Emory.

He let Franklin go without changing his expression but then turned and slammed his fist into his face. Franklin fell onto the unforgiving concrete floor and his head made a horrible thunk. I gasped involuntarily.

'He's okay,' Emory reassured me.

'Our definitions of okay are a bit different,' I retorted.

'He'll live.'

'Sure. Lucky boy.'

'We don't want him conscious in the car. Elementals can wreak havoc, even with their hands bound. Hopefully he needs a recharge and is nearly out of juice, but I don't want to risk it.' Emory picked up Franklin and carried him out to the Mercedes G Wagon. 'Gato, send him to the Common, and then you're in the back,' Emory said.

Gato nodded and touched his snout to Franklin's forehead. The tell-tale triangle faded.

'If Gato was going to send Franklin to the Common, you didn't need to punch him,' I pointed out.

'Oops,' Emory replied, unrepentantly. He pulled out a rope from beneath the lining of the boot, tied Franklin's arms behind his back and hogtied his feet.

'You've done that before,' I commented. 'Do you ever worry that we're the bad guys in this scenario? I don't think the good guys have people hogtied in their boots.'

'It depends on the narrative,' Emory said. 'He's the

one that burnt down five sites, the little shit.' He was angrier than I'd realised.

'You seem to be taking this personally.'

Emory opened his mouth and then closed it. He sighed. He couldn't explain.

'Is that because you're king of the creatures?'

Emory stilled, then he met my eyes and smiled wryly. 'I did say you'd work it out.'

'Hmm,' I agreed.

'This makes things easier. No creature is allowed to reveal our court, but now you know about it, it breaks the geas.'

I looked at him questioningly.

'The geas – the obligation for secrecy.' He sent me a rueful glance. 'The geas is now on you. You can't talk about it with a human. If you try, your magic will be forfeit.'

I blinked. 'No blabbing. Got it.'

Emory continued. 'The trolls and ogres aren't ruled by me. I didn't know about their fires – they hadn't reported them. The dryads told me about the garden centre, but they thought it was Common vandals. The gnomes' fire was only reported yesterday when I was somewhat preoccupied with Audrey and Cuth being sick. I haven't dealt with matters very well.'

I thought Emory was being a little hard on himself. He was only one man – dragon – whatever. 'The question is, is the virus a ploy to distract you from the fires, or are the fires a ploy to distract you from the virus?' I asked.

Emory shook his head. He didn't know, and he didn't like that one little bit.

CHAPTER 17

WITH FRANKLIN SECURED in the boot, we loaded up into the car. We'd taken one more look around the lab but nothing had jumped out at us. As we headed back to the Wirral, Emory took a phone call from Tom and explained about our detainee. Tom arranged to rendezvous with us at Chester.

We drove in comfortable silence for a while, each of us alone with our thoughts. Finally I asked, 'What's a flare party or an eternal flare?'

Emory grimaced. 'Benedict is psychotic. Elementals are on the human side, so I only have hearsay, but an eternal flare is a fire an elemental can make. It feels like you're on fire but you're not. You can burn forever without dying. In practice, the victims die of shock quite quickly. The mind can only take so much.'

I swallowed bile. 'That's sick. And a flare party?'

'Benedict throws punishment parties. He picks someone who has wronged him and he casts the eternal flare on them. As I said, I don't know for sure, but that's what we've heard. Elementals don't talk freely about him.'

'That's not strength,' I muttered. 'That's wrong. He should be stopped.' I managed to keep the accusation out of my voice. Emory was a king; he had a responsibility to the creatures, not to the elementals, but I didn't doubt he was strong enough to put a stop to Benedict.

Emory's mouth was in a tight line. 'I can't interfere in human politics,' he said. 'No matter how much I might want to.'

I got that, but when there was a monster acting in the world, they had to be stopped. All it took for evil to flourish was for good men to stand by and do nothing. I was going to do something about Benedict. Maybe I could sic Bastion on him – I felt like Bastion owed me, though he might not agree.

Silence fell in the car again.

We met Tom near Chester. Dark had long since fallen, but we decided against moving the unconscious Franklin from one car to the other. Instead, we car swapped: Gato and I hopped into Tom's Ford Explorer and he climbed into the Mercedes. Emory gave me a quick kiss on the forehead. 'I'm going with Tom. We'll pick up the papers the kid found and see where we're at.'

'I'll meet up with Hes and find out what she's dug up on Emma. Touch base tomorrow?' I asked.

'Of course. Amber DeLea is travelling up tonight. I'll be in touch to arrange for a time for her to scry the boy with the pin for us. Sleep well, Jinx.' He kissed me on the lips then hopped back into the Mercedes.

I fiddled with the settings in Tom's car and moved off. I was starving so I ordered some Chinese food to pick up from my local shop. I ordered enough for two in case Hes was about. If not, I'd love having Chinese for breakfast the next day.

The lights were on in my house when I pulled up in the drive. Hes was in, so no Chinese for breakfast, but I was relieved to have some company. Things were a bit mixed up in my head; it would help to talk it through, as much as I could with a geas on me.

'Anyone home?' I called rhetorically.

'I'm in here,' she shouted from the lounge. Gato and I headed in, carrying the takeout bags and she brightened when she saw them. 'Total win,' she commented. 'I haven't eaten yet.'

I grinned. 'Winner-winner-chicken-dinner.'

Hes grabbed plates and wine glasses, and I took a bottle of chilled white wine from the fridge. We ate while watching some trashy make-over TV, and I felt myself beginning to unwind.

'So,' Hes said, once we'd carted the empty plates back to the kitchen, 'what gives?'

I shook my head. 'Let's talk shop first. How did you get on with tracking down Emma?'

'We went to the office first and ran her through some credit checks. She's my kind of girl,' Hes said. 'She has a deep abiding love for shoes, which seems kind of funny for a mermaid. Anyway, around two months ago her shoe purchases stopped. All credit card use stopped. She owned a flat in the docks courtesy of her parents, so Nate and I decided to check it out. Nate phased us in, and we had a good look around. Clothes were still strewn everywhere – she obviously wasn't a tidy person. There were no signs that she'd been planning to leave, no packed bags. Her fridge was cultivating bacteria. Her cheese was furry.' Hes bit her lip, looking all of her eighteen years. 'I really hope she's all right.'

My lips tightened into a thin line. Man, I hated this aspect of my job. 'She's dead. That's how Nate could phase in without permission. The legal owner was dead.'

Hes's eyes went wide with shock and then filled with tears. 'Oh fuck,' she muttered. 'That sucks.' She brushed at her tears angrily and I looked away, giving her a moment to collect herself.

'Damn it,' she sighed. 'She was only twenty-one, three years older than me, but I got kidnapped and rescued, and she got kidnapped and dead. It just brings home how lucky I was.'

'Lucky – with an awesome PI after you,' I joked.

Hes grinned. 'Yes, there is that.' Her smile faded. 'We were too late looking for Emma.'

'She died around about the time I killed Ronan. Someone ordered a clean-up on Ronan's lab, and Emma was part of it. She was already dead when they burnt her body.'

Hes poured herself more wine and took a big chug. I tried to distract her from her morose thoughts. 'You're doing great at this private investigator in training.'

'It's so much fun snooping through people's stuff. You have to be nosey for this job.'

I grinned. 'So nosey.'

'So,' she smiled, 'since I'm so nosey … what's got you down?'

I rolled my eyes. 'I walked right into that one. I feel like the time is coming where I need to decide where I stand with Emory. He's an all-or-nothing guy. He's not pressuring me, but I still feel pressured. There are … complications.'

'What kind of complications?'

I sighed a little; damn this geas. 'Well, he's king of the dragons. If I date him, I have to be okay with being queen of the dragons – which seems ludicrous when I'm not a dragon. And I get the impression I'm not going to get a warm and fuzzy reception from his court.'

'Do you love him?' Hes asked simply.

I sighed again. 'Yes.'

Hes smirked. 'That wasn't so hard to admit, was it?'

'It was like getting a root canal,' I grumped. 'I've never said "I love you" to a guy, and I guess I'm still in denial. I know what I feel, but getting my head to line up with my heart is another story. I don't want to be a queen. I don't want people depending on me, looking to me. I can barely keep Gato happy.'

Gato let out a gruff bark, wagged his tail and laid his head on my knee. 'You think I could be a queen, do you?' He barked again. 'Thanks for the vote of confidence, big guy.'

'Ignoring all the queen stuff, if it was a choice of being with Emory or not being with Emory, what would you say?'

'I'd choose Emory all day long. But it's not Emory in isolation, is it? It's Emory the package deal.'

Hes wiggled her eyebrows suggestively. 'It's a pretty good package deal,' she leered.

That made me laugh. 'Yeah. It really is.'

'Has this helped?' Hes asked.

'I have no idea.'

'Right, I'll cross off "gives great love advice" from my CV tomorrow.'

'Talking about your skills… Did Nate phase you into the apartment, or did you phase yourself?' I'd been meaning to broach the topic of her vampiric skillset with her for a while; now was as a good time as any.

Hes frowned. 'What do you mean?'

'You know my dagger, Glimmer? It transfers powers.' Hes nodded in understanding and I continued. 'Mrs H had stabbed Nate and then you…'

'You're saying I have a vampyr's powers?' The girl was fast.

'I don't know for sure. You're Other now, so you've got to be something. Have you tried running since…?'

Hes looked away. 'I was really fast,' she whispered. '*Really* fast.'

I went into the kitchen and found a knife, nicked my finger and walked back into the lounge bleeding. 'Spit into the cut,' I ordered.

'Eww. Gross!' she objected.

'Vampyrs have healing spit. It's how they hide all the bitemarks.'

Hes made a face, but she spat into my hand. Shuddering a little, I wiped it over the cut. It just seemed wrong on some level to wipe spit into a wound. Then I wiped my finger clean: not a mark.

Hes swore. 'Fuck. How come I haven't wanted to drink blood?'

'You haven't become a vampyr because you're still living, you just have their skillset. You'll have to talk to Nate about it. He can teach you to phase, and they do a kind of hypnosis thing that might be helpful.' I realised then that I hadn't told Emory about the hypnosis. Something else to add to my to-do list.

Hes blew out a loud sigh. 'Great. More time with Mr Sexy while I try to pretend he isn't sexy any more.'

I grinned. 'He's still hung up on you, too,' I assured

her. I knew that he was, I felt it every time they were near each other. Today was the happiest I'd felt him since we'd been bound.

She brightened a little. 'Really?'

'Really.'

'Maybe I'll give him a call,' she said casually.

'You do that,' I agreed.

We called it a night and I locked up. I was just climbing into bed when my phone buzzed with a message from Mo: *The lab is owned by a shell company, which is owned by a shell company, which is owned by another shell company. It's a Russian doll. I dug deep. The last layer is Linkage LLP. I could only access information on one of the directors before my presence was found and I got kicked out. One helluva security system they have. The director was a Mr Stone.*

My stomach tightened. *Zachary Stone?* I messaged. *Gilligan.*

CHAPTER 18

I HAD STEAMY dreams and woke feeling a little hot under the collar. Abstinence when you have a sexy boyfriend is a lot harder than abstinence when you're single. I decided a run would calm my traitorous hormones, so I started my day with a brisk jog. Gato was delighted to join me, galloping around like a pup.

After our run and my shower, I checked my phone. I had a message from Emory. Amber DeLea was free at 9 a.m. this morning. He would bring her to my house. It was a good thing I'd woken early.

There was something about Amber that intimidated me: she was so together and strong. I looked round my mish-mash of a house. I bet Amber's house was like Lucy's, like an interior designer had styled each room. My house still had the neutral cream paint the last owners had slapped on. About the only homey touch I'd made was to put up the pictures of me and my parents. Well, it would have to do.

I had a head of a coven visiting me, so I thought I'd better break out the nice biscuits. I made a brisk trip to the Co-op and bought some her favourite blueberry muffins. Maybe she'd go easy on me if I gave her baked goods.

I didn't bother with makeup. Amber was going to scry the image of the little boy in the vision, something that didn't seem to be easy or pain free, though I hoped to be proved wrong.

I was just sitting down to some cereal when I realised Nate was close by. Really close. He phased into the kitchen out of the shadowy larder. 'Hey,' I greeted him.

He flashed me a huge grin. 'Morning, Jinx.'

My smile grew. 'You and Hes made up then?'

He flicked on the kettle. 'You could say that.'

'No wonder I had sexy dreams.'

'I waited until you were asleep,' he protested.

'It seems our bond follows me into sleep.' Nate blushed. 'Don't worry, my dreams were X-rated, but they were hazy. I'm getting better at my empathy all the time. I think I can work out how to drown out the bond a little sometimes so it's not so … present in our minds. We'll have to try it next time. Though I think distance will help.'

'Next time we'll be at my place,' Nate promised.

'Next time?' Hes called from the kitchen door. 'We're sure of ourselves, aren't we?'

Nate beamed at her, and the look they exchanged made me feel a little uncomfortable. They were going at this relationship thing full tilt, and I refused to admit, even to myself, that I was jealous with a capital J. Emory and I had stalled at kissing. Great kissing, amazing kissing, but still … kissing.

The doorbell rang. 'That'll be Emory,' I said, excusing myself to escape the cloying glances and touches.

When I opened the door, he was leaning against the door jamb. His green eyes locked onto mine, and his lips curved in a warm smile. 'Hey,' he said simply.

My heart fluttered, and I felt an answering goofy smile cross my mouth. 'Hey,' I replied. He leaned down and brushed my lips with his, lightly and full of promise, and something in me eased. I was making this way more complicated than it needed to be. I liked Emory. I loved him. I needed to roll with the punches and see where this went, or I'd never forgive myself.

'Enough with the lovesick glances,' Amber said from behind him. 'I've got a schedule. I'm not getting behind because you two want to moon at each other. Moon in your own time.'

I stepped back and led her to the lounge. 'Tea? Coffee?' I asked. 'I have blueberry muffins.'

'Coffee and a muffin would be great,' she admitted reluctantly.

Emory stood up. 'I'll get it,' he offered.

'Nate and Hes are in the kitchen,' I warned.

Emory gave no indication that he was upset at being

in close proximity to a vampyr.

'Taming him are you?' Amber commented softly. When I turned to her, she was staring at a photo of my parents. Her expression was hard to read, but if I'd had to guess, I would have called it regretful. Her eyes flicked to Gato. 'You seem to be doing well. All things considered.'

'I forgot that you knew them,' I said, gesturing to the photo.

'Yes.' She sighed and met my eyes. 'We weren't friends per se, but we were colleagues. We worked together a number of times. I hate black magic and I always try to root it out where I can. A lot of black magic takes away the free will of the enchanted.' Her jaw clenched. 'It's not right. Free will is something your parents also took very seriously since theirs was taken from them.'

'Faltease,' I said.

She nodded sharply. 'He made them Other, forced them and eighteen others into another realm they didn't choose and shouldn't have been part of.'

I blinked. I'd forgotten about the others but, if they were like me, maybe they could help me. The usual rules didn't seem to apply to me. If there was anyone else who could help me write a new manual, it would be another of Faltease's victims. I felt a glimmer of excitement. 'Do you know any of the others?' I asked optimistically.

'Faltease's fallen. I did.' She grimaced.

My heart sank. 'You don't know them now?'

'As far as the records show they're all dead.' *True.*

I sat down heavily, my eyes wide, my heart racing. For the first time, I had a motive for someone killing my parents. 'How did they die? The others?' I clarified.

'The first few reported deaths were accidental – car accident, fall during a hike, drowning after partying too hard, an overdose. Then there was a big fire that killed five of them after a night out. That was when alarm bells rang and the remaining victims went into hiding.'

'You said the records show them all being dead.'

'I said they went into *hiding*, I didn't say they did so successfully. Though your parents did far better than anyone else.' She frowned. 'Dammit, I was friendly with your parents, so I'll tell you this for free. I was told to give you this information.'

'Why?' I asked.

'I don't know the motivation for sure but, if I had to guess, someone wants you distracted.'

I swore. 'Distracted from the virus,' I guessed. 'Who told you to give me this information?'

'The witch symposium member, Sky Forbes.' Her tone was matter of fact, like that was that, like she hadn't just pulled the rug out from under me.

Emory came in, virtually at a run, carrying a tray of hot drinks and muffins. 'What's up?' he asked, sending a dark look at Amber. Nate must have said I was upset.

I did my best to send him a reassuring look, but his concern didn't lessen. Evidently I wasn't convincing. 'Tell you later,' I said.

Nate walked in and glared at Amber, too. 'None of that,' I said firmly. 'She's helped us a lot. I may not like it, but none of it is her fault.'

Nate tilted his head, considering my words. 'Okay,' he said finally. 'I won't rip her head off her shoulders.'

Emory growled, 'If anyone is ripping heads, it's me.'

'If anyone is ripping heads, it's *me*. I do my own head ripping. I'm a big girl.'

'I'll poison you all with an airborne virus before *any* of you can rip my head off.' Amber sipped her coffee calmly. *True*. Her comment was entirely too pointed.

Fuck. Airborne. I *knew* the injections had been a trial. I'd hoped the virus had to be injected, but it looked like whoever was behind this had wanted a smaller sample first, to test its efficacy. Perhaps the virus hadn't been finished before Ronan's lab was shut down. After all, no one had died yet except for poor Emma. I met Amber's eyes. 'Do you know a lot about airborne viruses?' I asked casually.

I saw a flash of approval in her eyes. 'I might do.'

'What can you tell me about them?'

'Absolutely nothing.' *True*.

Because it was on my mind, it was obvious to me. 'She's under a geas,' I stated.

Amber smirked a little and took another sip of her coffee.

'It's got to be the witch member, Sky,' I guessed.

Amber's smile widened. She didn't speak because she couldn't, but she didn't need to.

'Right,' I said, 'now we're cooking. My friend messaged to say Ronan's lab was owned by Linkage LLP. Anyone know anything about them?'

Amber sat perfectly still.

Emory pulled out his phone and dialled a number.

'Prime,' the voice answered. I recognised it as Ajay's.

'Linkage LLP. Tell me about it,' Emory ordered.

There was a pause. 'It's a company set up by the Connection to purchase all of their black ops sites,' Ajay said. 'All records of the purchase of those sites are carefully wiped, so there's nothing to link the Connection to anything less than sanitary.'

A rock settled in my tummy. The lab was owned by the Connection. Ronan's lab, the virus, all of it, was sanctioned by someone in the Connection. We had no idea how high this went.

Emory looked at me then said to Ajay, 'Who did you tell that I was going to the lab site?'

'No one!' Ajay's protest was instant and vehement. It was also one hundred percent true. Whoever had leaked that we were going to the lab, it wasn't him. The only other person we'd spoken to about the lab was Stone. I swallowed. I hated being wrong.

Emory finished his call, and Amber asked for a big bowl of water to scry in. I got her my washing-up bowl out of the sink, nothing but the finest Chez Sharp. To her credit, she didn't even blink. At least I'd washed out the suds first.

Hes joined the party and sat next to Nate. I put the bowl on the coffee table, with Amber one side of it and me on the other side. She opened the leather tote bag she always carried around, reached in and got out a few jars. She opened one, dipped in a paint brush and painted something cold and wet on my forehead. She used two other jars and painted two other symbols on my face. Then she looked at me. 'This will hurt.'

I knew that. 'Go ahead.'

'Think of the thing you want them to see. Think of nothing else,' she instructed, then reached over and painted a final symbol. As her last brushstroke finished, my brain felt as if it were exploding, like it was slowly being peeled back with a tin opener. I focused all my efforts into imagining the little boy. My head pounded. I dimly heard a whimpering sound but barely registered that it was coming from me.

I heard the sound of a phone's camera. 'Got it,' Emory said. 'End it,' he ordered Amber.

Amber reached over and used a baby wipe to wipe the runes off me, rubbing them out one at a time. Unfortunately it didn't wipe away my pounding headache. It looked like the pain was here to stay. I *knew* scrying wouldn't be fun. 'Baby wipe?' I commented to turn my attention away from the roaring in my head.

'Cheaper than makeup wipes,' Amber said evenly.

'You got it?' I asked Emory. He tilted his phone so I could see the image he'd taken. I could see the boy with the pin clear as day in the reflection of the water. 'Cool.'

'I'll send it to my people,' he said. 'See if we get any bites.' I knew now that he meant to more species than the dragons.

'No need,' Nate interjected. 'I know who he is.'

'Who?' I asked.

'Cathill.'

'The daemon?'

'The vampyr who was subsumed by a daemon,' he corrected.

I rubbed my head. 'But he got captured at St Luke's, right?'

'By the Connection,' Emory pointed out darkly.

'Fuck,' I swore. 'This is going to get messy.' I turned to Amber. 'I know you're under a geas, but say I have to go outfit shopping. Any places in particular it would be bad idea to go to?'

'Sorry, I don't know anything about the location – of shopping malls, I mean.'

'Well, do you think I should go shopping sooner or

later? Like today, or tomorrow, or the day after? Or could I wait to the weekend?'

'I'd go shopping by tomorrow,' she confirmed grimly. 'I wouldn't go the day after that.'

If I was reading her right, the airborne virus was going to be deployed within the next three days.

Time was ticking.

CHAPTER 19

WHEN AMBER LEFT, Hes and Nate also made tracks. Ostensibly they were going to research airborne viruses, but I think their research goals were a little different to mine. They were happy to leave the ball in my court while they focused on their own balls. I couldn't blame them; they were happy, and the virus was hypothetical for them. For Nate, it was a virus that could bring down his species' most hated enemies: dragons. Although he seemed to be all right with Emory, he didn't seem to be in a rush to save all of dragonkind. This was our deal and we'd sort it. Probably.

'What did Franklin's notes say?' I asked.

'We don't know. Franklin was still passed out. We tried to gain access to his flat, but it was runed up to the hilt. We'll need him conscious to gain entry.'

'We need those notes,' I said firmly. They were the key to the virus. Franklin had thought so, and after my initial assessment of him, he hadn't struck me as dumb. Young, weak, but not stupid.

Emory rang his second-in-command, Tom. Franklin

was awake in one of their safe houses, being restrained with magic-dampening cuffs even though he was in the Other realm. It felt like overkill, and I felt a little sorry for him. I'd had a run in with those cuffs, and they hadn't felt good.

Emory read my thoughts. 'We can't leave him unsecured. He could burn the whole place down.'

'I know, I know. It's just a little reminiscent of what Ronan did to us.'

'We're the good guys,' Emory assured me.

'Ronan thought he was one of the good guys, too. It's looking pretty certain that the Connection was behind his lab, so you can understand why he might have thought that.'

'He was dealing drugs to kids, and he was going to kill us,' Emory pointed out.

'I'm not saying he was a saint, I'm just saying the ends don't justify the means.'

'Don't they?' Emory said softly. 'Because there aren't many things I wouldn't do to save my people.'

'Could you kill me?' I asked. 'If that was necessary to save them all?' I don't know why I asked, because I didn't really want to hear the answer.

Emory opened his mouth then closed it again. 'I don't know,' he said finally.

I didn't blame him for that, though a part of me was sorry that I hadn't been given an instant 'no'. He'd lived quite a few more years than me, and that was bound to change his perception of things. He'd experienced far more than me, too – but that didn't mean I wasn't right.

'Tom said Franklin's awake so he'll bring him to his house now. Shall we meet them there?' Emory suggested, moving the conversation along.

'Sure,' I agreed.

Emory touched my arm. 'Are we okay?'

'Of course we are.' I gave him a playful punch on the arm. 'Let me grab some paracetamol for my headache and we'll roll.'

I took some paracetamol and some ibuprofen as well for good measure. Although I was downplaying it – my skull was splitting – but unfortunately we didn't have time for me to have a sick day. The airborne virus was going to be released in a couple of days; too much disruption and they might bring their plans forward. Urgency was the name of the game.

Whoever was behind all this was throwing all kinds of shit at us: the fires, the information about my parents. They wanted to distract us, so we had to focus now more than ever. Countless lives depended on it.

Gato hopped into the Mercedes and we set off. Emory directed me to a rough street in Birkenhead. It was a red-brick area with street after street of two-up, two-down terrace houses. Most of the residents lived below the poverty line. Despite the January cold, some of them were wrapped up, sitting out in the sun talking. Front doors weren't locked and, as we watched, people moved from one house to another. They might be out of work and down on their luck but they were part of a community.

A black Ford Escape parked alongside us. Tom nodded towards the nearest white PVC door. As we all got out, he walked closely behind Franklin to keep the neighbours from realising we had him in cuffs.

I was in the Other: the sky was purple and Franklin's house was *covered* in runes. 'What's your day job?' I asked him.

'Fireman,' he said, a little proudly.

I blinked. 'How does that work?'

He rolled his eyes. 'I can control fire. I don't need to have created it.'

'Huh. That's cool,' I admitted. 'So why all the runes?'

'It seemed sensible after stealing the notes.'

I frowned. 'It's kind of obvious though, isn't it? It basically shouts "Look, I've got something important here!"'

He glared. 'I don't have the financial resources to pay for enchanted runes.'

'Enchanted runes?'

'Invisible runes,' Emory explained. 'They're expensive.'

'Very expensive,' Franklin muttered. 'Affordable for the immortals who've spent several lifetimes doing nothing but gather wealth, but not so affordable for us mere mortals.' There was a lot of bitterness in his voice. The divide in the Other realm was deeper than I'd realised.

'We do more than get rich,' Emory replied mildly.

'Yeah?' said Franklin belligerently. 'Like what?'

'We support charitable causes,' Emory said firmly.

Franklin snorted. 'Sure. You make the world a better place.' *Lie.* 'Come on. Let's get this over with. You'll need me to touch the door while you unlock it,' he said pointedly, wiggling his cuffed hands behind his back.

Without changing expression, Tom tugged him forwards and smashed his face into the door. Franklin let out a low moan, and I felt sorry for him. It was disheartening that there was so much bad feeling between the species. When I'd first joined this realm, I'd learned that it had been ruled by the Unity. I'd foolishly thought that the new realm was more unified than the Common one. But wars and factions were rife within the Other realm, and resentment simmered under the surface all of the time, bubbling away, volatile and dangerous. Now it felt like the title 'Unity' was being used sarcastically.

With Franklin smushed up against the door, Tom unlocked it with his spare hand. Tom was not subtle, but he was effective. Voilà, we were in.

The house was small. The dining room at the front had a tiny table, and in the lounge at the back there was barely enough room to swing a cat. Everything about the dimensions was miserly. The lounge backed onto a small concrete yard. The walls were white and the carpets were beige. The only splash of colour was a music poster of a band I hadn't heard of.

'Where did you put the notes from the lab?' Emory asked.

He needn't have bothered. I could spot them a mile off. The poster bulged obviously in the middle. Franklin was a fan of the hide-behind-the-painting trope – except he'd done it badly.

Franklin gestured towards the poster but I was already moving. I untacked the bottom corners and reached up to an A4 wallet of documents duct-taped to the wall. Now wasn't the time to read them, and I didn't want to leave the house carrying something for the nosy neighbours to observe, so I tugged my shirt out of my jeans and stuck the notes in the waistband of my jeans.

'Paranoid much?' Emory teased.

'It's not paranoia when they really *are* out to get you,' I pointed out.

Gato suddenly let out a menacing growl and leapt towards the back door. He was directly behind it when it exploded inward, striking him and flinging him back into the wall. He landed with a thud and lay unmoving.

'Gato!' I screamed and ran to his side. His head was bleeding but he was still breathing. I turned in rage to the intruders and found myself unable to move.

'Isn't this fun?' a haughty voice called.

I couldn't turn to identify the speaker.

'Benedict,' Emory greeted him.

'Emory. You seem to have kidnapped one of my people.' Benedict spoke mildly but the malice in his voice was unmistakeable.

'Only when you ordered him to kill me,' Emory said just as calmly.

'You shouldn't have started sniffing round things that don't concern you, dragon. Perhaps if you'd focused on your own little species, you wouldn't have landed up here. I can't have you flouting my law and kidnapping my people – it makes me look weak. And we can't have that, can we?' He sounded like he'd taken a hard right at sane and driven right into insanity. Shit. The crazy ones were the worst.

I struggled but I still couldn't move.

'My pet wizards are holding your companions immobile, and you can't shift in this tiny little room,' Benedict taunted Emory. 'You're immune to fire but she's not, and nor is he…' he trailed off suggestively.

'If you leave the three of them alone, I'll come with you,' Emory promised.

'Three?' Benedict queried.

'The hound too.'

Benedict chuckled. 'It's just you I want, dragon. I've

got a beautiful flare party planned for you. Just because you won't burn under the fire doesn't mean you won't *feel* it.'

I finally found my voice. 'Emory! Don't! Fight them!'

'Stupid bitch,' Benedict snarled.

'Don't you fucking touch her!' Emory shouted.

Benedict stalked over to me, his pale, pock-marked face twisted in derision. The flames on his head danced and twirled as he sneered at me. The last thing I saw was his boot coming towards my face.

CHAPTER 20

M Y HEAD WAS pounding. Again. I reached up to my forehead and grimaced.

'Easy,' Tom advised.

My eyes opened, and I winced against the light. My thoughts were scattered and confused. I'd bet good money I had a concussion. What had happened?

'Emory?' I asked in panic, sitting up suddenly and making my world swim. Nausea rose in my gullet.

'Taken.' Tom's voice was grim.

I looked around. I was in my own bedroom. Gato lay next to me, still but breathing. 'Gato?' I asked. It seemed that one word was all I could manage.

'He'll be okay. He cracked his skull when he collided with the door but the witch healed it. She used his own magic to heal him so he's depleted. He just needs to rest.'

I took all that in. I felt depleted, too. 'How long have I been out?' I asked.

'Most of the day,' Tom confirmed.

Nate was reaching out to me, and I could feel his relief that I was conscious again. *I'm okay*, I tried to reassure him, but my head was hurting, and I wasn't sure if it worked.

Something drew my focus away from Nate. Something was prodding uncomfortably into my back. I reached behind me and pulled out the notes. At least they hadn't been taken. 'You didn't check these?' I asked, working hard to keep the accusatory tone out of my voice.

Tom's expression shuttered in the universal 'oh shit, I've dropped the ball' expression.

'I've been focusing on locating Emory,' he said finally. 'That would have been much easier if you'd already mated.' His tone was accusatory; tempers were running hot. He was frustrated, and I couldn't blame him. Emory had been taken on his watch.

'Why would it make a difference if we'd been mated?' I asked.

'True mates bond, like you and the vampyr. If you were mated, you could tell where Emory was and if he was dead or alive.'

I looked out of the window to give me a moment to collect myself. I hadn't considered for one moment that Emory could be dead. He was a dragon, an immortal dragon; sure, they could be killed, but they were tough. I had to believe that we had time, that we could rescue him. God, we *had* to rescue him. I still hadn't told him that I loved him. I felt useless and helpless and tears welled up. I dashed them away angrily, and Tom's expression softened. 'Sorry,' he muttered.

I swallowed past the rock in my throat and nodded briskly in response. Even that movement hurt. 'Drugs?' I asked.

Tom gestured to my bedside table at some white packets. I guess nothing can beat Common paracetamol and ibuprofen. I took a couple of each and hoped they'd help soon.

Darkness was falling outside. Benedict seemed the type to start a party in the evening, so I had to hope that he hadn't started torturing Emory yet. I was dangerously close to losing it, but I couldn't, not now. Emory needed me to focus.

I looked at the wallet, pulled out the notes and scanned them. They were as clear as mud to me, but at the last page I stopped. I recognised the writing. The i's were dotted with big juvenile hoops. I searched my memory. Where had I seen that in recent times?

I frowned suddenly. Uh-oh. At Arrowe Park Hospital, the nurse who had signed us in. Surely there were others in this world who wrote like that, but I didn't believe in coincidences.

'Tom, we have a problem. A big one.' He looked at me questioningly. 'I recognise this handwriting. The nurse at the hospital wrote like this – or very similarly. I can't say for sure it's hers … but damn, it can't be a coincidence. You need to get your creatures out of that hospital right now. She's not on our side, and she may not be the only one.'

He swore darkly, pulled out his phone and stalked out of the room as he dialled. I pushed myself out of bed and swallowed hard as the world swayed and I struggled not to vomit. Yep, concussion. I reached into my bedside drawer for an antacid – and there lay Glimmer. Silently, innocently.

I snorted. 'You're not fooling anyone,' I told it. I brushed past it and popped some pills out of the packet, but I hesitated as I closed the drawer. Finally, I reached into it and picked up Glimmer. 'All right,' I said. 'You can come.' It burst into song. 'If you're quiet,' I said firmly. Its song muted.

I slung on a jacket, put Glimmer in the pocket and headed downstairs. Tom was still on the phone. 'All of them,' he was saying. 'Every last one.' He hung up.

'How many dragons do you have locally that could help rescue Emory?' I asked.

'It's not that simple,' Tom replied.

'He's their king,' I protested.

'Because he's strong. If his court learns he's been taken captive by an elemental…'

'He didn't get taken, he gave himself up for us.'

'For you,' Tom corrected. *True.* 'And that's another thing we can't let his court know. You're his Achilles' heel. He wouldn't thank me for advertising it.'

'So who can we take?' I said, exasperated.

'The brethren are loyal to Emory,' Tom said firmly, 'but we're mortal. We're a little faster, a little hardier, but we can't breathe fire or shift. We're fire resistant but not flame retardant.'

'So what you're saying is that we're up shit creek.'

Tom grimaced. 'We need a location. Let's worry about getting a force together when we know where he is.'

I pulled out my phone and saw several worried texts from Nate and Hes. I let them know that I was all right. That wasn't the complete truth, but I didn't have time to deal with them right now. Then I dialled Mo's number.

'Hey, Jinx,' he greeted me warmly.

I didn't waste time with niceties. 'I need help – it's an emergency. I need you to find all the UK properties owned by Linkage LLP. Price is no object, but speed is essential. Be careful.' I'd dip into my inheritance if I needed too, as long as Mo was fast.

There was a pause. 'I'm on it,' he promised softly and hung up. That's one of the reasons I like Mo, besides the fact that he's easy on the eyes: he is brief and to the point. And skilled. I was confident he'd dig up a location for me. But now I needed something else; I needed someone on the inside. Two 'someones' sprang to mind.

I dialled Roscoe's number. 'Jinx.' His voice was low

and serious with none of its usual exuberance.

'Are you at Rosie's?' I asked.

'No, I'm not home.' *True.* 'I'm in Wales,' he said. *Lie.* 'I'm sorry, Jinx, I can't talk just now.' He hung up.

Fuck. I'd bet my left arm he was with Benedict. Roscoe knew I was a truth seeker. He wasn't home and he wasn't in Wales. He was trying to help me; my gut said that by 'home' he meant England. That meant he was in Scotland. Probably.

I texted Mo. *Focus on Scottish properties first.* I got a thumbs-up emoji right back.

I bit my lip. Maxwell was all the way in the Home Counties, too far away to help. That meant Roscoe and Maxwell were both out; that meant I needed to find another fire elemental. Only one sprang to mind, and she didn't have much reason to feel warm and fuzzy towards me.

I opened up my laptop and dug through my closed files. I still had a contact number for Mrs Bridges, the fire elemental I'd caught having an affair with a water elemental a few weeks earlier. I dialled her number.

'Hello?' she answered breathlessly and with a lilt as if she'd just been laughing.

'Mrs Bridges?' I asked.

'It's Miss Friars now. I'm getting a divorce.' She said it happily, like she was announcing she was buying a house.

'Oh, erm, congratulations?'

'Thanks. Sorry, who are you?'

'Um. I'm Jinx. I'm the PI your husband hired to confirm the affair.'

There was a heavy pause. 'Well, I can't say I appreciate the spying, or the pictures you took, but it turns out you set me free so I won't hold a grudge.'

'Thank goodness for that because I need a fire elemental's help.'

'You'll have to go to Benedict.' She hung up. Fuck.

I rang again. She answered after five rings but didn't speak.

'Benedict is the problem,' I said. 'I'm going to get rid of him.' The silence stretched. 'I need your help,' I pleaded.

'I don't know if I *can* help,' she whispered.

'Please. I'll pay you. I know Benedict is scary, but I promise I'll make sure this doesn't come back on you. You're the only other fire elemental I know. Kind of.'

She snorted. 'You don't know me at all.'

'Please,' I repeated. I wasn't above begging. 'Benedict has my boyfriend. He's planning a flare party for him.'

'Shit. Okay, okay. I'm still in Cressingham. I'll text you the new address.' She hung up. Moments later, my phone beeped with her details.

I forwarded the text to Nate and asked him to meet me there in thirty minutes. I made sure to phrase it as a request rather than an order so he could refuse if he wanted to. I got an affirmative back almost instantly. He was a good friend.

I turned to Tom. 'I'll have a location soon. Get a brethren team prepped. Have you got everyone out of the hospital?'

He nodded.

I grimaced. 'It will show that we know something is hinky at the hospital, and it will show that all the creatures are working together, or at least communicating with each other. But it can't be helped. We can't leave the patients there if it's not safe.'

'What are you going to do?' Tom asked.

'I'm going to get us some firepower.'

Literally.

CHAPTER 21

M RS BRIDGES – excuse me, Miss Friars – had gone down in the world. Her last home had been palatial; her new home was a flat. Despite that, when she opened the door to me it was clear that she was happy.

'I'm Jinx,' I introduced myself. 'My honour to meet you.' I touched my hand to my heart and gave a little bob. A little formality couldn't hurt.

'Samantha Friars, my honour to meet you, Jinx.' She returned the gesture. She was in the Other; I knew because she had a triangle on her forehead, but the biggest clue was the flames dancing on her head. 'Come on in.'

The flat still had a pile of boxes against one wall. 'Excuse the mess. 'I still haven't finished unpacking in my new digs.'

'And it's too small to do so,' a voice from the lounge bitched. I tensed.

'My partner,' Samantha explained. 'Bianca Symes.' That was the water elemental I'd caught her having the affair with.

'I told her to move in with me,' Bianca complained, standing to meet me. 'But she thought it would put too much strain on our budding relationship.' She snorted. 'We've been friends for years.'

'But lovers for only a few months,' Samantha pointed out with an eye roll. It was clearly an argument they'd had a few times.

I grinned and held up my hands. 'I'm not getting involved with this one.'

'Yes,' Bianca snarked, 'you just get involved with taking pictures, don't you?'

I winced.

'Bianca,' Samantha chastened, 'you said you'd behave.'

'I *am* behaving. I haven't dunked her.'

'I'm sorry,' I said, 'but it's my job. I get hired to find out the truth. If there was nothing to be found then I wouldn't have found it. But listen, I'm not here about you. I'm here for Benedict.'

Bianca's expression darkened. 'That homophobic piece of shit,' she muttered. 'He's a sadist, too. That isn't strength. The fire elementals have put up with his craziness for too long.'

'You haven't even met him,' Samantha retorted. 'He's charismatic and terrifying. You defy him and you die.' She met my eyes and I read the fear in hers.

'I swear he'll never learn that you helped me,' I tried

to reassure her.

'What do you need?'

Best to warm up to the big stuff. 'Can you tell me what happens at a flare party? How many fire elementals will be there?'

'There are usually ten or fifteen elementals, max,' Samantha said. 'Sometimes fewer. Benedict likes to make it feel exclusive. He enjoys "rewarding" his closest allies with the finest parties. There'll be a lot of other guests from all walks of life, though. He likes fine food, whores, drink.' Her face twisted. 'And all the while, someone is screaming in the middle of the room. Everyone ignores it, like it's not a sentient being screaming in front of them. No one objects.'

I swallowed, feeling bile rise in my throat. Benedict was vile, but I tried not to judge the bystanders. They were scared probably, terrified. 'Of those present, how many of them truly support Benedict?'

'Honestly? Maybe a handful are truly loyal to him, those he has elevated in our ranking system.'

'Ranking system?' I asked.

'I'm a three, in the middle of the elemental pack. It means I'll never be a member of our governing body, the Pit. Only fives can rule. Normal ranking is based on your magical strength alone, but two of Benedict's closest allies are only threes. He has declared them fives and put them on the Pit.'

'Packing the court in his favour,' I muttered. She nodded. 'And if I can kill Benedict, will his supporters let us go? Will we face recriminations from the Pit?'

Samantha snorted. 'They'll probably give you a medal. Benedict's true supporters are die-hard, but the rest will be damn glad to see a change of leadership. It's been five years of fear and hell. It's the only reason I'm meeting you. If you can put an end to Benedict...'

'I'm going to do my damnedest,' I said firmly. And I meant it. Benedict was a sadist and a twisted fuck, and – most importantly – he had Emory. If I could, I'd see Benedict locked up in magical dampening cuffs for the rest of his life – but right now I couldn't trust the Connection to keep him contained. The Connection had supposedly captured Cathill, and yet here he was strolling around as a kid. So no, maybe cuffs weren't an option. But if Benedict had to die, I wasn't going to lose sleep over it – well, I probably would, but that didn't mean it wasn't the right thing to do. Benedict wouldn't go down quietly so it would be self-defence. I was fully prepared for that eventuality; in fact, I was counting on it.

My phone buzzed with a text from Nate confirming he was outside. I blew out a breath. Now for the hard part. I started slowly, 'I have a magic dagger. It can make someone non-Other become magical.'

'Glimmer,' Bianca whispered, eyes wide.

'Faltease used it to plunge into a magical being's heart

213

and then plunge into the Common person's heart to transfer power. Sometimes they died, sometimes they didn't. But I've found the situation doesn't need to be so dramatic. Just a nick, a taste of blood, can give someone powers. And it doesn't take them from the gifter, it just gives them to the other person.'

I took a breath and continued. 'I haven't been Other all that long. I've got some weapons in my arsenal, but fire isn't one of them. If I try to face Benedict as I am, I'm going to get broiled.'

'You want to stab Samantha,' Bianca said flatly. 'Hell – fucking no.'

'Bianca!' Samantha glared at her then crossed the room and poured a generous glug of vodka into a glass. She mixed it with cranberry juice and a few shards of ice. 'Anyone else want a vodka cranberry?' she asked, forcing herself to sound upbeat.

'God, no,' I replied. 'It's like treating a urine infection while you're creating it.'

Bianca laughed. 'Dammit! Any other day and I'd like you.'

I flashed her a quick smile. 'Back at you.'

Samantha took a steadying pull of her drink. 'Just a little stab?' she clarified.

'A nick,' I promised. 'And I'll get you healed straight afterwards.'

'You're a wizard?' Bianca asked.

I nodded. I was misleading her a little about the healing, but I didn't want to give them another reason to refuse to help me. I was getting rather good at misdirection.

'I'll do it,' Samantha said, setting down her empty glass. 'But you have to promise you'll never tell another soul that you got the powers from me.'

'I'm not eager for this to get around,' I confirmed. 'We'll all take an oath of silence. If it gets out what Glimmer can do, I'll have people left, right and centre trying to steal it from me. And I've got better things to do.'

'Like killing arsehole elementals,' Bianca pointed out.

'Like that,' I agreed.

'Hurry up then.' Samantha bit her lip apprehensively. 'Before I change my mind.'

I reached into my jacket and drew out Glimmer. It sang happily in my mind. It knew it was about to be used, and it sensed my intention. 'Just a little cut,' I cautioned it and felt it pulse in agreement.

Samantha held a shaking hand out to me. I cut across her palm and she inhaled sharply, but otherwise she didn't protest. I braced myself and cut into my own palm. I misjudged and did it a little too deeply. Hot blood welled up. 'Ouch,' I said, 'and oops.' Bianca handed me a wodge of tissues and I tried to stem the bleeding.

I didn't feel any different. When I'd taken Mrs H's

powers, they had slammed into me and ripped away the compulsion that Stone had set on me. Now I felt nothing. What if it hadn't worked?

'Let's get healed up,' I suggested. I headed to the front door. 'Follow me.'

Nate was lounging casually against his car. 'I need some healing,' I said.

'I figured.' He gave me a disapproving look. He'd felt my pain.

'Sorry, but healing now? Samantha first.' I gestured towards her.

'May I heal you?' Nate asked her politely.

Her eyes were wide. 'You're a vampyr. You can't heal.'

'Not officially,' he confirmed. 'It's not something that's common knowledge. May I?'

Samantha nodded. Nate took a hold of her hand, licked it three times and let her go. He turned to me. 'Your turn.'

I shook my head. 'Wizard blood, remember?'

He considered my words. 'What is between us will supersede that.'

'You *hope*,' I replied. 'We can't risk it.'

'No, but we can't risk you not being able to fight properly. If you go after Benedict, you'll have enough difficulties to face. Pain and blood loss don't need to be part of them.'

'Just spit into it,' I suggested, remembering Wokeshire doing just that when I'd been in his dungeons helping his daughter recover from Boost.

Nate frowned. 'That's considered very insulting, the worst of insults. Worse than the C-word and the N-word combined.'

'Insult away. It's the safest way to do it. I won't risk you.'

He grimaced but hawked and spat into my palm a few times until the cut healed and faded. 'Thanks.' I gave him a quick hug.

He squeezed me back. 'I'll stay here until you're done,' he promised.

The women and I headed back inside the house. 'Now we need to test this,' I said. 'How the hell do I make fire?'

Samantha stared at me. 'I don't even know how to explain it.' Her eyes were wide. 'It's like breathing to me.'

'You do it,' I suggested, 'and tell me what you're doing.'

A ball of fire appeared instantly in her hand. 'I just wanted it to be here and it is.' She looked at me apologetically. 'I'm sorry, I don't know what to say.'

I held out my hand and willed fire into it. Nothing happened. I frowned. 'Maybe it's like the IR,' I muttered. 'Do you imagine it in your head first?'

'I guess. I don't know. I just know what I want to

happen and it does.'

'No release word or anything?'

She shook her head.

I imagined a small candle flame appearing on the palm of my hand. I wanted it to be there; I *needed* it to be there. The small flame instantly appeared and danced on my skin. It was hot and I yelped as it burnt me. Reflexively I stopped the flame and stared at my palm where a blister was already forming. Damn.

'Oh shit,' Samantha wailed. 'I'm so sorry. You need to know your flame won't hurt you and then it won't. Your own fire won't burn you.'

I stared at the evidence to the contrary as she bit her lip. 'You weren't focusing on the fact that it can't hurt you,' she said. 'You need that in your mind too, as well as the fire. I'm sorry. It's so basic, I just didn't think.'

'No worries.' I kept my tone light. I didn't blame her; using magic was just like breathing to those who were introduced to it at a young age, but breaking it down was hard.

I took a deep breath and tried again. I held out my unblemished hand and this time tried to conjure a flame that wouldn't hurt me. Nothing happened. Burns *hurt* and my fear of pain was holding me back. Dammit. Emory needed me. He might already be under a flare, feeling a sensation like this across his whole body, and I was wimping out because of a burn the size of a twenty-pence piece. No, Jinx. Just no. Get your shit together.

I closed my eyes and pictured myself with a flame that wouldn't hurt me dancing on my palm. I felt a whisper of something on my hand and opened my eyes. Hot flames rose from my skin, pain and burn free. Relief flooded through me. It had worked.

Now I just needed to learn enough to face a deadly fire elemental with thirty-odd years' experience.

Easy as pie.

CHAPTER 22

I MAGINATION REALLY IS the limit. I hadn't grown up seeing all sorts of different fires as being par for the course. I hadn't seen orbs of floating fire or sheets of dancing flames; I'd pretty much only seen a fire in a fireplace. Conjuring and using different flames of different sizes and temperatures wasn't in my comfort zone, but I got really comfortable really quickly because there was no other option.

I studied Samantha's repertoire of flames against the backdrop of her warning. 'I'm only a level three. He's a level five. He's going to throw more at you than I can create.' I nodded my understanding as I wondered whether my limitations would be the same as Samantha's. Would I also be a level three? It didn't matter. Benedict wouldn't be expecting me to have any fire so whatever I had would give me an advantage. Maybe it would be enough. It had to be, for Emory's sake.

Finally, after a long hour, I drew a line under it. Mo had texted me three potential locations. I sent them onto Tom and let him do some preliminary recces. As I prepared to leave, I showed them to Samantha. 'Here.' She pointed to Castle Dunnottar.

'It's a ruin,' I complained after a quick Google.

She looked at me flatly. 'It is to the Common. The illusion and enchantments keep people away. Benedict is self-important – he'll definitely be at the castle. He loves to pretend he's the king of us all.'

I texted Tom that the castle was the most likely location.

Evening was drawing in, and I was feeling anxious. I stood up. 'I'd better go. Thank you so much for everything you've given me and shown me.' I just hoped it was enough.

Bianca sighed and scrubbed a hand across her face. It was obvious she was wrestling with something. 'I don't want to like you, Jinx. You ruined Sam's life. I don't want to like you, but I do. Give me the damn knife.'

I blinked. 'What?'

She rolled her eyes. 'You don't fight fire with fire.'

My mouth dropped open, and I felt extremely dumb. 'Water,' I said to the water elemental.

'Water,' she agreed. 'Why do you think our relationship is so taboo?' She gestured at Samantha. 'It's not just that we're both women but it's also because one wrong move on my part could destroy her. I can never relax, not fully. I always have to keep my magic in check. We can't even sleep in the same room unless we're both in the

Common.'

'So why haven't the water elementals done anything about Benedict?' I complained.

Bianca grimaced. 'If I had to guess ... bribery.'

I sighed. 'This realm is a shit tip.'

Suddenly Bianca grinned. 'Yeah, but it's *our* shit tip. Come on, we don't have all day. Let's slice and dice.'

We repeated the procedure, and Nate healed us both. He also healed my burn and I was grateful when the dull, throbbing ache slid away. When we headed back inside, he stayed by the car. The girls were pleasant to him, but no invitation inside was forthcoming. I felt a little bad about leaving him out in the cold again.

'I guess we don't have time for a full tutorial,' I said regretfully.

'No.' Bianca sighed. 'Let's just check it works.' She conjured a ball of water in her hand and heated it until it steamed. Then she cooled it until it formed a hard ball of ice.

'Cool,' I breathed.

'Your turn. And yeah, you need to imagine that it won't physically affect you, especially if it's steam or ice.'

I was prepared this time. As I concentrated, a sphere of water appeared in my hands and I let out a squeak of triumph. I wanted it hotter and hotter, but not to feel the heat. I grinned when it turned into a wall of steam that did no more than caress my skin. I cooled it until it became a massive shard of ice. I could feel that it was cooler, but it wasn't an icy penetrating cold that would give me frostbite.

'Now try to do fire,' said Bianca.

I blinked at the 180-degree turn, but did as she suggested. The fire orb appeared instantly. She sagged in relief. 'Thank goodness. I wasn't sure if one person could contain two elements, especially opposing ones. It's never been done before.'

'There have been wizards who could primer all four elements,' I pointed out.

'Yes, *primer* them. They still had to have the external element. You have it internally. Trust me, it's different.'

'If you say so. Thank you for this, Bianca. You may well have saved my life,' I admitted.

'Just make sure you end *his*,' she entreated grimly.

I nodded but made no promises. My number-one priority was rescuing Emory; everything else could go to hell. Though if I had my way, Benedict would be going there too. I went to give the women handshakes but was pulled into a group bearhug.

'Kick his ass,' Bianca murmured to me. 'Then come back one day soon, and I'll show you how to be a level-five water elemental.'

'Thanks.' I drew back suddenly. 'Hey, has my hair changed?'

Samantha grinned. 'Same old boring brunette,' she

reassured me. I was relieved; the flames looked cool on Samantha's head, and the watery locks looked ace on Bianca, but I loved my own hair. It seemed like my humanity was clinging on.

I said goodbye and went out to Nate. 'Are you okay keeping this to yourself?' I was careful to phrase it as a question rather than an order.

'Your secrets go with me to the grave,' he promised.

'I'm not sure that promise holds as much weight with an undead person,' I teased.

He grinned back. 'It's all you're getting.'

My smile faded. 'Listen, are you up for this?' I asked him. 'I could use some backup, but I know rescuing dragons isn't your deal. I won't blame you if you want to sit this one out.' *Lie.* Oops. My subconscious thought I would probably blame him a little.

'I'm your friend, Jinx. Of course I'm coming. I'm going to help you to rescue Emory, even though he's a dragon. I'm ignoring that now he's your ... boyfriend. And he's not all that bad – he's actually quite a decent bloke. And Jinx, I appreciate the restraint you've shown. You've done your damnedest not to order me around, even though we have a controlling bond. I'm conscious you could have me following you around all the time singing a theme song, but you don't. You don't take advantage of a situation that most would. So, yeah, I'll come. I'll rescue your dragon willingly. That's what friends do.'

I was momentarily speechless, possibly a first for me, and my eyes welled up. I blinked the emotions away and punched him on the shoulder. 'Thanks,' I murmured.

He grinned at me. 'Come on. Let's get on the road. Scotland is a long way.'

'Meet me at my house,' I suggested. 'I'll sort alternative transport.' We both got into our cars and moved off. Normally I'd have suggested carpooling, save the environment and all that, but today I wanted some privacy. I had calls to make, and I didn't want witnesses.

First I called Tom. Our conversation was brief. I asked him to arrange a helicopter to Castle Dunnottar and he said it would be at the green near my house in an hour. He would arrange another helicopter for the brethren, and we'd meet at the castle. He was business-like and focused, and I liked his can-do attitude. It was especially handy when planning a rescue attempt to save your boyfriend from nefarious clutches.

Next I called Lucy. I was insanely grateful when she answered on the second ring. 'Can you talk privately?' I asked.

'Mostly,' she replied. 'Though Esme hears everything you say, too. But she says she won't repeat it. There you go, we're as private as we can be.'

'Thanks, Esme. Guys, I need advice. Emory has been kidnapped and—'

'What? Are you all right? Do you need me and Esme to come and smash some skulls? Because we will absolutely be there.'

'Thanks, but we think he's in Scotland, and it'd be difficult for you to get there in time. And we're on a tight schedule. But now you know about the Other, I can talk this through with you. You remember Stone?'

'How could I forget Inspector Sexy?'

'Yeah, well, when we first met he used magic to compel me to trust him. I found out about it and cut ties with him.'

'That'd be a big deal for anyone, but especially for you. You already have trust issues.'

'Thanks,' I said flatly.

She snorted. 'It's not a secret. Everyone who's met you knows you have trust issues. I bet you and Emory haven't even had sex yet.'

That derailed my thought process. 'What's that got to do with anything?'

'You gotta trust someone to have sex.'

'No, you don't. I've had sex with people I barely know,' I protested.

'Sure, a one-night stand. But this is different. This is a relationship, and you've got to trust the other person before you … you let them in.' Her tone was thick with innuendo.

I didn't want to talk about this right now. 'Jeez.

You're distracting me. We're talking about Stone. There's some evidence he might be involved in my current case. There have been some poisonings when Stone was in the vicinity. It may be coincidence, but it doesn't feel like it. However, my gut doesn't feel he's knowingly involved although someone in the Connection is. But I've been fooled by him before. What if it's not my instincts talking to me but a leftover from the compulsion or something?'

'Didn't the compulsion break?' Lucy asked.

'Yeah. Big time.'

'Then I'd say whatever you're thinking, it's your gut. Trust it.'

It was what I wanted to do, but I'd wanted someone else to reassure me that it was the right thing. 'Okay. So loop Stone in?'

'I would,' Lucy confirmed. 'He seemed pretty capable, and he might be what you need during a rescue attempt. You are going to rescue Emory, right?'

'Obviously,' I replied, affronted.

'All right. Kick ass and take names,' she instructed. 'But be careful, Jess.'

'Thanks. Love you, Luce.'

'We love you too.'

'We?'

'Esme. She knows I love you, so she loves you too. Wolves are pretty straightforward creatures. You're part of our pack, even if you're not a wolf.'

That made me grin. 'I've considered you pack for quite some time,' I replied. 'See you on the other side.' I rang off.

Next I dialled Stone. I half-hoped he wouldn't answer but he did. 'Jinx. Are you okay?'

'I've been better. Are you alone? Can we talk?'

'I'm alone in my car,' he assured me. 'What's up?'

'Emory has been kidnapped by Benedict. Benedict *is* behind all of the fires. He was making his fire elemental, Franklin, do them under threat of death.'

Stone swore extensively.

'There's more,' I continued. 'Ronan's lab developed the virus that's been making a lot of the creatures sick. A few of them were injected with the virus while you were present.'

'I swear I don't know anything about the virus.' *True.* 'And I didn't see anyone being injected.' *True.*

'I said you were present, not that you saw it. You were in the vicinity. And there's still more. After we dug through some shell companies, we found that Ronan's lab was owned by Linkage LLP.'

There was a long pause. 'That's the Connection's company,' Stone whispered finally.

'Yes. Someone in the Connection is trying to bring down the creatures. Benedict's little flambé session is bound to be connected. All of the targets were creatures.' I didn't say anything about Stone's father being one of the directors of Linkage LLP; being the boss on paper didn't mean that Gilligan knew the inner workings of the company. He could be wholly ignorant of the injections. My gut disagreed, but either way, now was not the time to bring it up.

Stone sighed. 'There's a lot of anti-creature sentiment in the Connection,' he admitted. 'But I would never have expected it to get to this. Our unity is the Connection's strength. If we lose the creatures, it's going to be a cluster fuck.' *True.*

'It is,' I agreed. 'So I'm rescuing Emory and stopping Benedict. Maybe we can find out who is behind it all, but if not, I'll settle for destroying Benedict.'

'Benedict – he's unhinged. I'm coming with you.' Stone could primer fire, which might be useful. Besides, the more the merrier as far as I was concerned.

'You have half an hour to get to my house in Bromborough,' I said. 'Or the helicopter will leave without you.'

'Be there in twenty.' Stone hung up.

I rang Bastion. He didn't speak when our phones connected. 'Hello? Hello?' I barked. 'You have awful phone manners. I haven't found the mastermind yet, but I've found the middleman. Want to help me take them down?'

'Where?' he responded finally.

'Either meet me at mine in half an hour, or at Castle

Dunnottar in three hours.'

'Castle.' He rang off. He wasn't the chatty type.

I felt better. I had Tom, I had Stone, and I had Bastion. I also had fire and water. What could go wrong?

CHAPTER 23

I ARRIVED HOME with time to spare. I looked down at my clothes: jeans, T-shirt and a leather jacket. I swopped the jeans for black combats that would allow greater ease of movement. I swapped my trainers for flat leather boots with a solid sole, the better to kick someone with. I had Glimmer and my flick blade. I didn't worry too much about my lack of arsenal; this fight wasn't going to be won with the usual weapons. I did, however, put my lockpicks in one of my pockets. They often came in useful, and I felt naked without them.

Gato was still resting. He stirred and tap-tapped his tail when he saw me, but he didn't move more than that. He was going to sit this one out.

I'd been in the Other for two whole days without hopping out for a recharge at night. With hindsight, that was an oversight; I'd never had to go more than a day between charges and I had no idea of how much power I could use before being catapulted back to the Common. I thought of all my experiments with fire and water and hoped I hadn't used up all my magic resources before the fight had even begun.

In the stillness of my house, I let myself worry about Emory. I hoped Benedict was the type to keep him safe and well until the party started. My gut clenched to think of Emory being captured by such a sadist, but I couldn't think like that, couldn't let myself be distracted. We were going in to rescue Emory and kick Benedict's ass. Then we were going to find out who was pulling Benedict's strings and stop an airborne virus from being released God knows where, by God knows whom. Totally doable. No sweat.

I kissed Gato, checked again that I had Glimmer and left. Nate was parked on the drive – and so was Stone. They were eyeing each other warily.

'Let's go,' I said firmly and led the way to the green. We'd been there for all of a minute before we noticed the helicopter. It came in virtually silently; it wasn't the one I'd ridden in before. This one must have had spoilers in the main rotor blades and tail rotors to reduce the noise.

The pilot was Chris, the one who'd flown me before. He gave me a nod, his eyes grim. There was none of his youthful exuberance; he knew that Emory had been taken. I nodded back and settled into my zone.

It wasn't long before the boys started talking. I mostly tuned them out and watched the world pass beneath me until darkness descended. I had nothing but my thoughts to turn to, and they were dark, filled with worry and recrimination. Why had I been waiting to take that next step with Emory? I loved him. I ached with it, I was terrified of it, and now I regretted I hadn't done something sooner. Well, no more. After I'd rescued Emory – and I refused to think of an alternative – I was going to tell him how I felt. I wasn't going to let myself hold our relationship back. So what if we were mates? It didn't take away my free will if it was my choice to be with him. And damnit, I did choose him. Now we just needed to live long enough to do something about it.

The night was clear and the moon was high. I saw another grounded whirlybird as we came down to land. I couldn't see the castle, and I hoped we weren't far from it. I checked my watch: 7 p.m. That was soirée o'clock in my world, but I hoped to hell that Benedict was an 8 p.m. guy.

We set down next to the other helicopter, opened the door and hopped out. Our helicopter was a commercial one, but the other was a Chinook. I couldn't see how many occupants it had, but I knew it could take about fifty-five people. That reassured me. This wasn't just me and my dog breaking in – though I missed my dog – this was an organised team. Of soldiers, I hoped.

Tom got out of the Chinook with a blond guy and they eyeballed Stone and Nate with open hostility. 'Stow it,' I said firmly. 'We need them both. They bring different talents to the party, and I'll use everything in my arsenal to get Emory back, even if it's your enemies.'

Tom jerked his chin towards Stone. 'You trust him? Because if you're wrong, we're walking into a trap.'

'I haven't told anyone about your location,' Stone promised. *True.*

I didn't know if Emory had told his people about my truth-seeking abilities; I guessed not, since he was so pushy about keeping them hidden.

'Emory trusts my instincts,' I said firmly and with as much conviction as I could muster. 'Stone is the poster boy of the Connection. If there's anyone here who's part of the Connection, he'll recognise them. You and I wouldn't. This is more than just a rescue. We need to dig out this whole thing so it doesn't fester. That's what Emory would want.'

The muscular blond was glaring at me. 'You're not the Prime's mate. Why should we listen to you?'

Tom stayed silent and let me field that one. I wasn't sure if that was because he agreed or because he wanted to see how I'd deal with it. I remembered Emory's advice: if I was to be a part of his court, I had to show strength.

I glared right back. 'I *am* his mate. And you should listen to me because I'm the bitch that's getting him back.'

Tom smirked a little. 'You're finally accepting it.'

I shrugged. 'I'm stubborn.'

Tom grinned. 'We noticed.'

For the good of everyone, I ignored him. 'Do we have any idea where Emory is being held in the castle?'

The blond man hesitated and looked again at Stone and Nate before he spoke. 'The intel is patchy,' he admitted unhappily. 'We managed to get some suggestion that the "party" will start at 8 p.m., but some said later at 10 p.m. We believe Emory is being held in the top tower of the castle, but it's heavily guarded at all levels. If we can get to him before the party starts, we can fight our way out. But if the party's started, it'll be a bloodbath – for all of us.' His tone was matter of fact. He wasn't fazed at the thought of a bloodbath but I was; I didn't want to be responsible for leading sixty-plus men to their deaths. But for Emory, I'd do it.

Tom pulled out some pictures of the castle. It wasn't the ruin I had seen via Google. The tower looked to be about four storeys high, with a flat, castellated roof. He also showed us a floorplan with the ballroom circled. If a party had been organised, it would be here.

'The easiest way in is from above.' I was thinking aloud. I turned to the helicopter pilot. 'Do you have a parachute or two in there?'

He raised an eyebrow. 'Two.'

I looked at Nate, who nodded in response. 'Nate and I will skydive onto the tower and make our way in from the top.' I paused then spoke directly to him. 'Will you be able to get in or do you need permission?'

'I've checked. It's a commercial property and not a home. No permission needed – we're good.'

'Great.' I turned back to the others. 'So while Nate and I are accessing the tower to get Emory, you guys need to create a loud diversion to draw away the guards. Explosions would be good. Do you have any explosives with you?'

Blondie grinned at me. 'You're skydiving in, and you want us to set off a bunch of explosions in an ancient, carefully restored castle?' He turned to Tom. 'I'm warming to her.'

Tom's lip twitched. I think he had already warmed to me.

I scanned the dark sky. There was no sign of Bastion, but I didn't want to wait. If the party was starting soon, I had to get to Emory before Benedict started flinging around his horrendous flare fire. 'No time like the present,' I said. 'Have you got a communication system we can use?'

'Have we got a communication system?' Blonde snorted. 'Toots, we've got the Rolls-Royce of systems.'

'Don't ever call me Toots again,' I said firmly.

'Yeah? Or you'll do what?' he taunted.

I glared. 'I'd threaten to stab you with Glimmer, but the truth is I'm not stab-happy. I'd probably dye your hair pink and spread malicious rumours about your sexual prowess.'

'Christ, I'd rather be stabbed,' he muttered. He pulled out two radios and attached one to me and one to Nate. 'These are AN/PRC-126 radios. They're used primarily for two-way radio telephone communication among special-force team members when they're in combat.' He ran through the operational basics and emphasised the need for radio silence. We were only to use them when we wanted to rendezvous after we'd rescued Emory.

'What's your name, Pink?' I asked.

'Greg Manners,' he replied.

'For someone called Manners, you're very rude,' I pointed out.

'Yeah, I get that a lot,' he conceded with a cheeky wink. 'See you on the flipside, Toots. Give us ten minutes' head start.'

I glared again at the ludicrous nickname. 'Sleep with one eye open, Manners,' I warned him. The banter steadied me as I suspected Manners had intended, but it wasn't going to stop him getting pink hair. I believe in delivering on my threats.

Our helicopter pilot, Chris, handed Nate and I our parachutes and we stepped into the rigs and fastened the leg and chest straps. I checked the altimeter and then checked Nate's Automatic Activation Device, AAD, and turned it off. We were jumping a HALO jump, high-altitude, low-opening, so we didn't want the AAD to fire. Nate toggled mine to off as well.

'You good with opening at 2,500 feet?' Nate asked.

I agreed, though I'd never pulled at less than 3,500 feet before. I guessed the theory was the same; there was just a lot less time under canopy for us to be spotted or shot at. I ignored my nerves. Emory needed me to be hot on it tonight.

The occupants of the Chinook moved out and started towards the castle. They were heavily armed with guns and knives. They wore camouflage uniforms and they moved like they knew what they were doing.

One of them stood out like a sore thumb: Franklin. Tall, weedy and determined, he was cuff-free now and it looked like he was joining the side of the righteous. I wished I'd had the chance to talk to him, to be sure there was no chance of a double cross. I had to trust Tom's instincts about him, and that was hard. Yeah, I have trust issues.

Tom and Manners smeared some greasy camo paint on and joined the tail end of the group. They were moving out quickly but I barely heard a sound. We gave them ten minutes and it felt like an eternity. Finally, Chris hopped up and started the helicopter's engine.

We climbed in but didn't bother securing our seatbelts. 'It's a still night,' Chris called. 'Scarcely any wind at all. I'm going to drop you almost on top of the castle, so I'm taking us up to 15,000 feet before we approach.'

'Roger that,' I replied. The engine was shockingly

quiet.

It didn't take us long to level out. 'We're at height. Ready when you are,' Chris called back.

We opened the helicopter door and cold air rushed in. I normally wear a helmet when I'm skydiving, and it was weird to be without one. I redid my hair, tying it as tightly as I could. Luckily we had visors, albeit cheap plastic ones. They'd have to do.

We weren't wearing jumpsuits, so we didn't have shoulder straps to hold onto each other. 'Arms?' Nate suggested and I agreed. He's a far more experienced skydiver than me, so I was happy for him to call the shots. I'm significantly lighter than him, so jumping together in formation would help us arrive at the target at much the same time.

'We'll go head down to start, then get stable and flat-fly down. Keep it simple. I'll pull first, then we'll spiral down, right toggle.'

'Okay.' I wasn't feeling as nervous as I'd expected. I was focused on Emory and we needed to go.

Nate and I faced each other in the doorway, shoulders towards the exit, then we grabbed each other's arms and jumped out of the helicopter. My stomach lurched like I was on a rollercoaster. Normally when you jump out of a plane it is flying forwards so there isn't this lurching feeling. Under any other circumstances I'd have been enjoying myself; I'd always wanted to jump out of a helicopter.

Nate squeezed me, and we arched our backs and flattened out. The cold air was whistling around us. It was the first time I'd skydived in the dark. My depth perception was out of whack, and I couldn't see the ground properly. This wasn't feeling like my best idea.

Nate checked his altimeter and let go of me before turning and tracking a little distance from me towards the castle. Then he waved off, pulled his parachute, and I followed suit. I checked my parachute; it was big and beautiful and something in me eased. I guessed a subconscious part of me had been worrying about another sabotage attempt.

Light poured from the castle windows, all the better to light our way and prevent the occupants from seeing us. I pulled down my toggles in a practice flare and steered to the castle. When I was virtually above it, I pulled on my right toggle enough to start the downwards spiral but not enough to stall the canopy.

Nate was already landing. He did it perfectly and turned and bundled up the canopy so it wasn't in my way. I followed suit, turning into the lightest of winds and letting go of the toggles. If I flared too early or too late, it wouldn't go well.

I flared a little too late, hit the rooftop with a bit of a thud and rolled. I lay there for a moment with the wind knocked out of me.

'All right?' Nate whispered.

I stood up. I'd be bruised tomorrow but nothing was broken. We bundled the parachutes roughly back into the rigs and removed them. We were good to go.

I drew Glimmer, more for something to do rather than with the intention to use it, then I felt the tiniest breath of wind. It made me turn – and there was Bastion.

One moment he was a huge terrifying griffin, the next he was the man I recognised. He was no less terrifying. 'I took care of the guards on the roof earlier,' he said by way of hello.

I blinked, not really wanting to know what he'd done. 'Thanks?' I queried. I peered into the shadows of the roof and spied a foot poking out. I was glad not to have witnessed his rampage; I'd seen the depth of Shirdal's destruction at Ruithin Castle, and that had been quite shocking enough for one lifetime.

'Let's go.' Bastion gestured to the doorway.

Nate pulled at the door. 'Locked.'

I tried to use the IR to open it but nothing happened. 'The IR's not working,' I said, hoping it wasn't a sign that my magic was already failing me.

'Invisible runes,' Bastion grunted. He reared back as if to kick open the door.

'Wait! Let me pick the lock,' I argued. 'It'll be quieter. We want stealth until we've got Emory.'

I picked it in under a minute. Bastion was first

through the door and I heard a gurgle as the guard died. He wouldn't be the last one to die tonight.

Ready or not, Benedict, here we come.

CHAPTER 24

W E MADE OUR way to the first door. It was locked, but the mechanism was a joke and I picked it easily. We entered the room: no sign of Emory. Bastion left us to open the other four doors while he went out to deal with any guards. We opened each door on our level amid the sounds of bloodshed and violence as he cleared the way. Still no Emory. Our intel was sour.

An explosion rocked the castle, quickly followed by another. The cavalry had announced its presence to draw away the guards so we could get Emory, but Emory wasn't here. All we'd done was announce ourselves and lose the element of surprise. Fuck. If Emory wasn't here, he was at the party and we needed to get there. Now.

I turned to Nate. 'We need to get to that party. Phase us.' Then I instructed Bastion, 'Fly to the ballroom.' He was a professional assassin: he would have done a recce of the castle first and know the location of the ballroom.

Bastion nodded and launched himself out of a window, transforming into a griffin as he fell. If he hadn't brutally murdered my parents, I might even have admired his skills.

Piggyback,' Nathan said to me.

'What?'

'I can use vampyric speed if I'm carrying you. Get on my back and let's go.'

I sheathed Glimmer and jumped onto his back. He caught me easily and I put my arms round him. This was not dignified in the slightest. I was the worst badass ever.

As Nate ran into a shadow at speed, my skin prickled and flashed freezing cold. Then we were out of the shadow before he plunged us into another one. We moved through the castle faster than I could have ever imagined, but my bones were aching with a deep abiding cold that felt like it would never leave. My teeth started to chatter. Great way to help with a discreet entrance, Jinx.

Finally, we phased out of the icy shadows and into the light of the ballroom – and there was Emory. Discretion went out of the window and rage came instead.

He was cuffed to a wooden post, burning with flames that didn't mark him. His body was battered and bruised, and he had deep cuts all over his torso. His face was contorted, and he was panting with pain, but he was trying not to give Benedict the satisfaction of seeing him scream.

I screamed instead. Rage, hot and boiling, like nothing I'd ever felt before, swept through me. I would *not* lose another person I loved. Not ever – and certainly not like this. I gathered the water within me and poured a river of it over Emory's body. The flare flames stuttered and died. 'Heal him!' I roared at Nate.

I turned to Benedict. 'I'm going to kill you, you son-ofabitch,' I raged at him. *True.*

I was so focused on Benedict that I barely registered the other 'guests'. People were screaming and some were fleeing, but I scarcely noticed. My focus was the scarred little fuck who hadn't got enough hugs as a child.

I conjured white hot flames from within me and threw them towards him. Benedict's eyes widened in surprise, and he ducked out of their way. His panic suggested he wasn't fire retardant if the flames weren't of his own making. Good to know. My flames struck the wooden chairs he'd been standing in front of and they instantly started burning fiercely. One of his lackeys stepped up and spread his hands.

I saw Roscoe and Maxwell. 'Help me!' I demanded. Then I spotted Franklin. 'Help us!'

Franklin may not have felt warm and cosy about us kidnapping him, but now he was on our side, and he'd seen the writing on the wall. He was Benedict's tool and he'd be discarded when his usefulness had played out. We were his only hope of freedom.

Franklin, Roscoe and Maxwell stepped up to the plate and battled against the die-hard Benedict fans. I narrowed my focus to Benedict himself and everything else washed away. Enough was enough: enough terrorising his own people, enough flare parties – just *enough*. I imagined a flame-thrower's flame, straight and hot, and flung it right at him. He ducked again and this time I struck curtains, which exploded into a massive blaze. Damn – I'd have made Benedict toast if I'd caught him with that bad boy.

'Clear the room!' I shouted. 'Get everyone else out of here.' I hoped they'd all listen to me, including Emory and Nate. I couldn't afford to be distracted, and I didn't want to risk barbecuing a bystander, no matter how not-quite-innocent they might be.

The element of surprise had worn off, and now Benedict was retaliating. He stood, legs akimbo, and drew his hands together in a whirling motion. Flames shot out and grew, spiralling and twisting and writhing. He created a tornado of flames and directed it towards me.

I had a moment of panic, and my mind went blank. I dimly registered Emory roaring my name, his voice laced with fear. I blocked it out and my mind cleared. I couldn't withstand Benedict's flames, and there was very little in the rapidly emptying ballroom to hide behind.

You don't fight fire with fire.

Bianca was a level-five water elemental so I hoped her skillset could beat Benedict's, even when applied by a weak novice like me.

The fierce tornado crackled ever closer and its heat

slammed into me. Dimly I thought that Emory would like how warm it was. Then I imagined a curtain of water, a constant deluge pouring all around me, a cascading waterfall that surrounded me from every angle. I willed it, and so it came to be. The water thundered into existence, splashing against the marble ballroom floor – but still Benedict's inferno swept towards me. I could just about see it as my watery veil started to obscure my vision.

I thought again about Bianca and Samantha. When they had come together, it was steamy. I focused on the water around me and willed it to not harm me as it got hotter.

Benedict's blaze struck my waterfall and the flames sizzled and hissed. I flung the water outwards, pouring it forwards. Steam rolled when the elements met, filling the ballroom with a thick fog. The remainder of the water that hadn't turned to steam continued to pour down, flooding the floor.

The battle between the elements continued until finally Benedict's flames succumbed to the water. I felt some temporary relief at my success, but as I looked around, I noted that the sadistic bastard had melted into the fog.

I squinted into the wall of whiteness. It wasn't normal fog, it was fog combined with the smoke from the fire, thick and heavy – super fog. Great. I was stumbling around blind. Then inspiration struck, and I edged closer to a window. The water I'd poured everywhere covered the marble floor and I splashed loudly as I walked. Fuck.

Near the window were the burnt remains of the chair. A charred leg would do. I grabbed it and smashed the sixteenth-century glass, then I gathered my intention. I let out a breath. 'Grow,' I ordered the breath, making it become a wind. Like Benedict had done, I made the wind swirl and whirl, and I sent it around the ballroom, funnelling the smoke and fog out of the smashed window.

It took only a minute before it started to lift and I saw Benedict, crouched low and quiet in a corner, waiting to make his move. Our eyes met and I didn't hesitate. I touched the ankle-deep water swirling around me and willed it to become ice, ice that didn't hold me. It held Benedict, however, locking him instantly in place.

He swore darkly as I skidded towards him with significantly less finesse than Torvill and Dean. Benedict's hands lit up with flames as he tried to melt the ice around him. I reached inside one more time and looked for water. I poured a stream at Benedict and snuffed out the flames around him, but unfortunately his work with the flames had already succeeded and he flung himself out of the way.

I blew out a breath and used it to primer air to lock him into place, like his pet wizard had done to me in Franklin's house, then I immediately called water again and poured an unrelenting torrent of it at him. It struck him with force.

As I poured water over Benedict, Glimmer sang, *'More!'* I made the water colder until Benedict could hardly move, then colder still until it coalesced around him as ice. I kept it around him, cold and unrelenting. His internal fire stuttered and died, and his heart with it.

In that moment, I felt no remorse. He had hurt so many, killed so many. He made others live in fear because of their sexuality or because they'd looked at him the wrong way. No, I felt no remorse, no regret.

I stalked forwards and warmed one section of the ice so I could lean forwards and touch his pallid skin. I dropped the air, dropped the water. It was done.

I closed my eyes and let myself breathe, seeking my inner calm and the ocean within me. I let the ocean sounds silence my surroundings and I sought the truth. Who was behind this virus?

Gilligan Stone nodded. 'Kill the obstructive Prime. Nothing can interfere with the release this Saturday.'

'And the bitch?' Benedict said eagerly.

'No.' Gilligan frowned. 'Leave her. My son is fond of her. He wouldn't let her death go uninvestigated.'

'And we must care so much about what young Zachary wants,' said a mocking voice. It was from a woman marked as a member of the symposium.

'We don't want him making this his personal crusade,

Sky,' Gilligan snarled. *'Nothing can jeopardise the release, not even my son.'*

Where will the release happen? I quested urgently, but nothing came. I'd had my one answer from the dead and there would be no more.

I tried to find my way back to myself but I was lost. I started to panic. I'd sent everyone away and Gato was at home, far from my side. Who would bring me back to myself? Fear gripped me.

Love came. It wrapped around me and caressed me, soothing the panic. I was safe and I was loved. Hands were touching me, stroking my face, but though I was aware of them I couldn't *feel* them. I needed to feel the hands, the love.

I willed myself back to my body and wrenched my eyes open. I met emerald eyes. 'Hey,' I managed.

'Hey.' Emory smiled.

'You rescued me,' I said.

'You rescued me first,' he countered with a lopsided grin.

The world wobbled and my skin started to itch. 'Gilligan Stone and Sky Forbes. The release is Saturday, but I still don't know exactly when or where,' I managed to say.

My skin was so itchy that it felt like it was on fire. I took another breath – and then the Other kicked me out of its realm and into the Common.

CHAPTER 25

MY HEAD WAS pounding and I felt a strange sense of déjà vu, but this time Emory was there when I clawed my eyes awake. Although his arms were around me, he was arguing with someone. I squinted and saw Stone. 'Enough shouting,' I moaned. 'My head hurts.'

Emory looked at me in surprise. 'You should have been out for hours.'

'How long has it been?'

'Twenty minutes tops.'

I was exhausted but their shouting had drilled through my fatigue. 'Anyone got a paracetamol?' I asked jokingly. I felt half-dead. I was trying to be upbeat but, man, I felt awful, like I'd been hit by a bus. Everything *hurt*.

Bastion stepped forwards in his human form again holding out a small black bottle no bigger than my thumb. 'Drain it,' he instructed. He might be an assassin, but I was pretty sure he knew that Emory would kill him if he harmed me. And my head *hurt*.

I drained it. The taste was surprisingly pleasant and

sweet, and the sugar hummed on my tongue with something else. Warmth pushed through me from my head to my toes and I instantly felt better, pain free and rejuvenated. It was a full-on miracle in a tiny, sinister-looking bottle.

I brightened. 'Cool. Thanks.'

Bastion nodded.

Emory was looking at us, eyes wide. 'Did you just give her your final defence?'

Bastion didn't respond. Emory's jaw dropped. I was missing something.

'The potion you drank will bring an injured soldier back from the brink of death,' Emory explained. 'It is incredibly expensive and highly prized, especially by the griffins. The witches only make a single batch of it every few years. It could be ages before he can get another final defence.'

I looked at Bastion. He stared back at me, his eyes revealing nothing. What the hell? Why on earth would he give something so precious to me? My radar hummed. 'Thanks,' I repeated with a little more feeling. I sat up in Emory's lap.

We were still in the castle. 'What's the sitrep?' I asked.

Manners stepped forwards. 'We have remarkably few casualties. The majority of the fire elementals sided with us against Benedict. Your friend Roscoe has been promoted by popular vote. The other guests found themselves other places to be. We took note of all of those attending but we didn't have the authority to contain them.'

'Where are we with Gilligan and Sky?' I asked.

'We're trying to ascertain their location.' Manners admitted.

I checked the time. 'It's nearly 9 p.m. on Friday night. We don't know when the virus is going to be released on Saturday, but the odds are it will be somewhere busy in rush hour, around 9 a.m. or 5 p.m. If it's the former, we don't have time to waste. What are you arguing with Stone about?'

Stone was pale and palpably shaken. 'I wanted to contact my father, ask him where he is. They don't like that idea.'

'Why not?'

'Because we don't trust him,' Manners explained slowly, as if to a small child.

'You don't have to. I do,' I said firmly to Manners and Emory.

Emory nodded slightly.

'Call your dad,' I said to Stone. 'Say you want to meet up to discuss … marrying Elvira. He'll bite.'

Stone met my eyes ruefully. 'Yeah, he would at that.'

'Call him.'

Stone looked at Manners then at me. 'You're in the Common, you won't have access to your powers.'

Ah. In the Common I could tell a truth from a lie if I was there in person; in the Other I could tell even over an electrical medium. Stuck in the Common as I was, I wouldn't be able to tell if Gilligan was lying to his son.

'We'll have to risk it,' I said finally. 'Time is ticking.'

Stone pulled out his phone and dialled his dad, Gilligan. It rang out. So much for that bright idea. I turned to Tom. 'Have you found anything helpful about the virus in the castle?'

'Thankfully, yes. In a safe we found something marked "virus" and something marked "antidote". We're keeping the antidote refrigerated and flying it to our scientists for testing before we give it to the current victims.'

I blew out a breath. 'Well, that's something. If it *is* the same virus that's being released, we could potentially manufacture more antidote for any more victims, right?'

Emory shook his head. 'Not in the time frame we'd need. To reverse engineer something like that would take months, maybe even years.'

Things were never simple. 'Well, it's a start,' I said. 'Better than nothing.'

Stone's phone rang. 'It's my father,' he said. The room fell silent as he answered and put the call on speakerphone. 'Father, thank you for returning my call.' He spoke rather formally.

'What is it, Zachary?' Gilligan's tone was warmer

than his words suggested.

'Elvira.'

'Yes?'

'I think it's time.'

'Finally,' Gilligan crowed with triumph. 'Let's celebrate with a drink.'

'I won't be home for another couple of hours,' Stone said.

'I'm a night owl. Come over when you're done.' Gilligan hung up.

'What is it with everyone's terrible phone manners?' I muttered. 'Where's home?'

'Ragowrie Castle.'

Emory turned to Tom. 'Get Chris to prep the chopper. We're not done yet.'

I wanted to have five minutes with Emory, mostly to reassure myself he was okay. 'Can we have five?' I asked softly. Emory stood and put an arm around me. We excused ourselves and went into a study, kicking out its sole occupant to get some privacy. Alone at last, I wrapped my arms around him and hugged him tightly. His torso was still bare, and he was covered in dried blood.

'That was scary,' I said finally.

'I didn't enjoy it,' Emory agreed.

'Let's agree to not let you be kidnapped again,' I suggested.

'Deal.' He gave a half-smile, but his eyes were haunted, and I hated to see that look in them, hated to wonder what had been done to him to put that look there. I needed to chase it away. Forever, if possible.

I leaned down to kiss him but he drew back. 'I've definitely got prisoner's mouth. It's like morning breath but worse.'

'I don't care.' I kissed him, and this time he let me. It was soft and gentle, a homecoming. We were both exhausted, and our kisses were slow and tender, meant to reassure rather than ignite passion.

Eventually Emory pulled away. 'We need to get going.'

I nodded. 'Yes, we do. I love you.'

He froze. 'What?'

'I love you, Emory. Sorry it took you almost dying for me to say it. I'm going to work on that.' I frowned. 'Apparently I have issues.'

Emory was smiling. 'You love me.'

'I do.'

'I love you too, Jess.' The kiss this time was on the wild side of raunchy and suddenly we were in danger of needing a room.

Someone knocked on the door. 'The chopper is lifting off in two minutes,' Tom called. It was like a bucket of ice.

'Okay,' Emory replied. 'We'll be there.' He turned to

me and raised an eyebrow. 'Shall we see it through?'

'We've started, so we may as well finish,' I agreed.

We went to the helicopter and climbed in. It looked like both whirlybirds were coming along for the jaunt. I snuggled up with Emory. Nate, Tom and Stone were along for the ride but Bastion had excused himself. I closed my eyes and let myself rest. Sleep took me.

I AWOKE WITH a jolt when the helicopter landed and Emory squeezed me reassuringly. 'I'll phase us into the castle as Stone's back-up.'

I blinked. 'Don't you need permission to get inside?'

Emory shook his head. 'I've been experimenting. It turns out that's an undead issue. I'm still very much living.'

'Thank goodness,' I muttered.

Stone left the helicopter first and headed up the long gravel driveway to his father's castle. We gave him a head start and then followed. The castle was small but perfectly formed. It had turrets. Who doesn't love a castle with turrets?

Stone entered and we phased into the shadows, staying unseen. We followed him, flowing in and out of the icy shadows, hidden in the darkness. My teeth started chattering again. Man, I hate phasing.

Stone knocked at his father's study door. 'Father?' he called. There was no answer. Stone pushed the door open and gasped as he rushed in. We followed.

Gilligan Stone was swinging from the chandelier, his face ashen and fixed in surprise. Dead.

Stone ran to him and grabbed his legs, as if to lift him up and let him catch his breath. I stepped forwards. 'He's gone, Zach,' I said gently.

Stone made a choking noise and shook his head in denial. He went on holding up his father, as if he could bring him back by sheer strength of will, and my heart ached for him. I knew all too well what it was like to find your parent dead. I stepped forwards. 'He's gone, Zach. Let's get him down.'

'I can't let him go,' Zach said, emotion choking his voice.

I understood. 'I'll help. Get ready to catch him,' I said softly.

I imagined a sword of fire, like I'd seen Stone use once before. It was awkward because I wasn't quite tall enough to reach, so I straightened the chair that had been kicked over and stood on it. I used my fiery sword to cut through the heavy rope that hung from the chandelier.

Stone caught his father's body as it fell, carried him tenderly and laid him down on the sofa in front of the fire. He ran a hand over his father's face and closed his eyes. Another voice spoke from the shadows. 'He gave me his notebook about the virus. About the planned release.'

'You!' snarled Stone, whirling around. 'You did this!' He flicked his lighter and his sword of fire appeared. He leapt towards Bastion, but then Emory ran with vampiric speed and tackled Stone from behind. He held him back.

'I talked to your father,' Bastion agreed. 'He didn't want to be arrested, didn't want to be dishonoured. He chose this path.' *True.*

'He would have done the right thing!' Stone cried. *Lie.* The lies we tell ourselves are often the worst ones, but sometimes we have to lie in order to cope. Stone's father was dead and gone; pissing on his grave was cruel and unnecessary.

'He did,' I said softly, as if to a scared child. 'He told Bastion what we needed to know. Your father did the right thing in the end.'

Stone nodded. He clenched his jaw, struggling to regain his usual lack of expression, but his poker face was full of holes and I could see his grief and shock clearly.

Emory released Stone carefully, keeping an eye on him lest he dive for Bastion again, but Stone stood immobile and broken. Lost. I felt a pang of sympathy in my heart.

Bastion flipped to the salient pages and handed the notebooks to Emory. Emory paled. 'Ten viral bombs spread across the country. We need to move. Now.' He gave Stone a searching look and murmured, 'I am truly sorry for your loss.' *True.*

Stone gazed back at him, hunting for any sign of insincerity but he found none. He nodded in silent acknowledgment.

Bastion opened a window. 'You and I are not done!' I called to him.

He met my gaze. 'When my daughter is well, we will talk.' He jumped from the window.

'I hate it when he does that,' I muttered.

'We've got to go,' Emory repeated urgently.

I turned to Stone, but before I could say goodbye, Emory tugged me into his arms and phased us out of the castle and into the grounds. Another phase and we were next to the helicopters again. 'We've got a problem,' he said.

CHAPTER 26

GILLIGAN'S NOTEBOOK WAS very specific both about the locations and the detonator mechanism. The book looked brand new, and if I had to guess, I'd say that Gilligan had written it that day. He had realised what was happening when Stone rang, and he'd made his own call. To me, it was the cowardly way out; he should have faced up to his actions, not ended his life because of them. Stopping the viral bombs, though, might redeem him. I hoped so for Stone's sake.

The bombs were set to go off at 9 a.m. Because there were multiple locations, Emory called in more brethren teams. They were briefed and tasked to stop the explosions up and down the country. One of them was in Edinburgh, from which we were only half an hour away by helicopter.

Emory looked at me questioningly and I nodded. Sure, we'd see it through. We were all tired and worse for wear, but the clock was ticking.

Emory being Emory, he called ahead to the location of the bomb, a pub on Rose Street in a busy shopping district. I guessed it had been too hard to place the bomb in Edinburgh Castle and thanked goodness for small miracles.

Emory affected a posher than usual British accent and stated that a bomb threat had been called in to the police. The bar needed to evacuate immediately and we, the bomb squad, would be there shortly to secure the scene. I guess he wasn't confident about his Scottish accent.

The two choppers set down on Rose Street. It was busy and bustling and people gawked at us landing in such narrow confines. The bouncers from the pub, Bobby's Bar, were doing everything they could to herd people away and I could see the panic in their eyes. Bombs weren't in their job description.

The brethren moved out like military. Still armed, dressed in black and with camo paint, no one argued with them as they set up a perimeter and pushed away the civilians. Manners, Tom and I headed in. As Emory started to follow, I held my hand up to his chest, which was sadly now clad in one of Tom's spare shirts. It looked like he was wearing his dad's clothes. 'Stop,' I ordered. 'You're a—' I lowered my voice '—dragon. You're vulnerable to this viral shit. I'm not, Tom's not, Manners is not. We'll go in. You man the perimeter.'

He glared and clenched his jaw but a moment later he reluctantly agreed. 'You're getting all the fun tonight,' he groused.

I sent him a ridiculously flirty wink. 'The night is young, boyo.' My Welsh accent was terrible.

Emory shook his head. 'No,' he said firmly. 'Never do that again.' But he was smiling, and the shadows in his eyes were fading. I blew him a kiss and went inside.

The bar was eerie now it was empty. I glanced around; from the lack of our people in there; the bomb was probably in the basement. I followed the sound of the others. Manners and Tom had already located it by the time I stumbled down the dark stairs. Manners glanced up at me.

'Don't mind me,' I said. 'I'm just sightseeing.'

He snorted, ignored me and turned back to the device. It was cylindrical with lots of wires, and it looked like it belonged in a movie. Tom and Manners had Gilligan's book open and were poring over it. As they carefully followed its painstaking instructions, I caught myself snoozing. It had been a helluva rocky ride, but watching them was like watching paint dry. In the movies, deactivation was over in a dramatic five-minute countdown; for us, the process took well over half an hour.

Finally Manners called out to me, 'You want to do the honours?'

I yawned. 'I'm not a glory hound,' I reassured him. 'This is your gig.'

Manners gave me a little nod that meant something

that I was too tired to decipher. He turned back to the device and moved the top of it. It clicked. He and Tom grinned and did a man hug with much back slapping, so I guessed the day had been saved.

The device was stowed in bag, then the bag was put in metal case and locked shut with an external combination lock. They were taking it seriously, and rightly so.

'Good work,' I commented into the gloom. 'Let's roll.'

We went back up the stairs. Manners gave a nod to Emory and that was that: no cheers, just a silent acknowledgement of a job well done. Emory gave a sharp whistle and all the men climbed back into the helicopters. The 10 p.m. revellers at Rose Street gave us a drunken cheer as we set off. I waved and felt like a queen. Maybe I could get used to this gig.

We set off for home, and this time I stayed awake. Tension remained high throughout the flight as we waited for feedback from the other nine teams that had been sent to disable the other bombs. Team by team they checked in, until finally the last one had called in. Our relief was palpable.

But the bombs weren't all Gilligan had given us. There was a new lab up and running that needed to be destroyed. I called Roscoe and asked for a favour. He promised grimly that the lab would be destroyed when it was empty, and all the computers and notes would be destroyed too. He would take anything marked as an antidote and eradicate anything viral. If in doubt, he would destroy everything. We had to do all we could to prevent this happening again.

Finally our helicopter landed on the green near my house. Emory surprised me by following me out. 'I'm not letting you go yet,' he said.

I smiled. 'Good, but erm … I'm pretty shattered so… Cuddle and bed?'

'Sounds good. But maybe throw in a shower, too.'

Even with Tom's shirt, I could still see blood splattered on his arms. The January air was crisp and biting. 'Man, you must be freezing.'

'I'm looking forward to a hot shower,' he admitted. 'And food.'

We walked hand in hand back to my house. I didn't hear the chopper lift off again, but I knew we were alone. I opened the house and called up to Gato, who came down the stairs yawning. I beamed at him. 'Hey, boy. You missed all the action.'

Emory kissed my shoulder. 'I'm going to grab a shower while you fill Gato in.'

'I'll start some food. Frozen pizza?'

'Sounds great.'

Remembering the warmth of Audrey and Cuth's house, I turned the heating to max. I hoped they would be given an antidote soon because It would kill Emory if they didn't make it.

I cooked four pizzas. I might manage to eat an entire one – I have a pretty good appetite – but Emory would have to polish off the rest. God knows when he'd last been fed by Benedict. That grim thought made me bite my lip, and I nearly threw in an extra pizza, but five would have been overkill by anyone's standards.

I gave Gato some love and attention and told him about our adventures. He listened attentively, wagging and barking in the right places. He was too smart to be called a dog or even a hound. He was more than my best friend, and I was relieved that he seemed so much better. He'd been listless when I'd left and I'd been worried. Sure, my worry for Emory had taken precedence, but my worry for Gato had been a constant hum in the background, like a toothache. We cuddled on the sofa together and the last of my tension drained away. I was home with the ones I loved.

Emory came down just as the pizza was ready wearing jogging bottoms and a T-shirt. He could make a bin bag look good. 'Smells good,' he smiled, reaching for the food. We switched on some music and chatted while we ate, deliberately keeping the topics light and fluffy. We'd had enough torture, murder and mayhem for now. We'd talk about what Emory had been through one day, but this wasn't the time.

When we'd both eaten our fill, I referred to the elephant in the room. 'Have we heard anything more on

Sky? Or Cathill?'

Emory frowned. 'Cathill is a ghost. We haven't seen anything of him since the battle at the bombed-out church. Obviously he's still around, but we were looking for an adult and it seems he's been running around as a child.'

I sighed. 'He can change his age at will, right?'

'That's right.'

'So he could be any age. He could be four or fourteen or forty.'

Emory grimaced. 'Yeah.'

'Then how do we find him?'

'I'm not sure,' Emory admitted. 'If we had something of his, maybe one of the witches could scry him – for a price.'

'Which brings us back to the witches. Besides Sky, did Gilligan give any more details about his henchmen in his notebook?'

Emory shook his head. 'Not really. He named Sky, but we've had our eye on her for a while. Do you remember Reggie Evergreen's death had a witch involved in the cover-up? Someone had doctored the police photos – enchanted them?'

I remembered. Amber had been concerned that it was a witch from her own coven.

'The brethren checked old CCTV footage from the police station,' Emory continued. 'It's backed up to the cloud and held for three years before being destroyed. Sky Forbes went to the police station just after Reggie's death. Etiquette dictates that she should have contacted Amber because she was in her coven's territory, but Amber confirmed that she never got a reach out. Sky was under the radar for a reason, and the most likely explanation is likely to be the true one.'

'Occam's Razor,' I agreed.

'Exactly. But we don't have any evidence against her, and the police visit is hardly the smoking gun we need. We can't accuse a symposium member with that.'

'Can we go after her with Gilligan's notes?'

Emory shook his head. 'I don't think so. We're trying to keep a lid on this. If we let it be known in the wider creature community that some of the human side were trying to kill them, there'd be a mass revolt. There's be no kowtowing to the Connection any more.'

'Would that be so bad?' I asked softly.

Emory grimaced. 'I ask myself that all the time. But I lived for 120 years without the Connection, and it was chaos. Vampyrs preyed on younglings, dryads killed anyone that damaged their trees, werewolves and vampyrs were fighting. There was death every day. Now we have peace. It may be built on lies, but at least we're *safer*. Together we are stronger.'

'But the creatures are all together under you.'

'That's a recent development in the last ten years or

so since I became Prime. I offered protection to the gnomes and they accepted and named me king. It kind of spiralled from there, and before I knew it, I was named Prime *Elite*, a title that's only been used once before, as far as I know.'

'But you're building something strong too, something that could stand up against the Connection.'

'Yes. There's a lot of anti-creature sentiment but I would never have thought it was this bad.' Emory ran a hand through his dark hair and shook his head slightly. 'I don't know where this leaves us.'

'Yes, you do,' I disagreed. 'We dig in and we see how deep it goes.'

Emory flashed me a smile which made me melt. 'I love it when you say "we".'

I smiled back. 'We make a great team.'

'We do,' Emory agreed softly. He leaned forwards and kissed me. 'Have I mentioned that I love you?' he asked.

'Just once or twice. I could hear it again.'

His lips curved against mine. 'I love you, Jessica.'

It was time to roll the dice. Maybe we were mates, maybe we weren't; there was only one way to find out. 'Do you know, I suddenly find myself with lots of energy. Have you got any ideas for a bedtime cardio workout?'

Emory studied me carefully. 'Are you sure? You know what it could mean? No take-backsies.'

'I know.' I let out a breath. 'I love you. I'm done running from this. I'm all in. You have my pure, unadulterated consent. Let's see where this goes.'

Emory continued to study me. 'You've had a hard few days. You have to be sure. This could be the start of a mating bond that will last our whole lives. I *want* to be with you for the rest of our lives, but if you can't say the same…'

I interrupted him. 'On a day like today, the rest of our lives seems like it might be too short. I love you, Emory. I feel like my heart is ripping out of my chest with love. I'm sure.' I kissed him softly and tried to regain a lighter mood. 'Now about that workout…'

Emory smiled slowly and seductively and I felt an answering pull. He leaned down and scooped me up into his arms as if I were feather-light, then carried me effortlessly up the stairs to my bedroom. 'I've got all kinds of workout ideas,' he purred.

Gato was lounging on our bed. 'Out,' Emory instructed. Gato looked back and forth between us and huffed audibly. He slowly got off the bed and went downstairs to sleep on the sofa.

Emory gently laid me down and then firmly shut the door. He turned back to me, his emerald eyes flashed with passion and purpose as he stalked towards the bed. 'You're going to be mine,' he promised, his voice gravelly and possessive.

'Yours,' I agreed, 'as long as you are mine.'

'Deal,' Emory agreed. 'This is going to be good.'

'Only good?' I teased.

'Earth shattering,' he countered.

'You're setting me up for disappointment,' I taunted, pulling the tail of the dragon.

Emory's smirk was predatory. 'You're not going to be disappointed, my love.'

I wasn't.

CHAPTER 27

I STRETCHED LANGUIDLY, basking in the afterglow of truly amazing sex. Endorphins do such good things to you. My muscles ached slightly, but it in a nice way. A lot of those muscles hadn't been used in a while. A very long while.

'You keep wriggling like that and you're going to wake the beast,' Emory murmured into his pillow.

I wriggled a little more. He reached for me and rolled over me in a smooth motion. There was no trace of the sleepiness that had been in his voice before as he pinned me to the mattress.

'Hi,' I smiled.

'Hi,' he replied, giving me a sweet kiss.

'I'm a little sore,' I complained.

'I give great massages.' He kissed my shoulder and my neck lightly.

His phone rang and I swore. He let go of me and laughed, but he still answered it. Apparently a king is always on call. Even when he was *on call*.

Suddenly he froze. 'So soon? Are they sure?'

I could hear the caller respond. Tom, I thought.

'Okay. I want to be there … in case. Can you pick me up in thirty minutes? From Jinx's.' Emory hung up. 'They're giving the antidote to the original viral victims. I want to be there when they give it Audrey and Cuth in case they react badly to it.'

'Of course,' I agreed readily. 'Do you want me there?'

He thought about it. 'No,' he said finally. 'You've probably got work to catch up on. I've had Tom wire you some money for the time you've spent rescuing me.'

'Along the lines of my current rates?' I asked firmly.

He looked away. 'Something like that.'

I frowned. 'I don't need to be bought.'

Emory grinned and kissed my frown lines. 'I know you don't. We're mates.'

'About that mating thing. Is there a ceremony we need to do or…?'

His lips twitched. 'I told you, the mating process is started once we have sex. There's no going back. Can't you feel it?'

'What?' I shifted against him, rolling my hips against his lower half. 'Can I feel that?' I said lewdly, giving him a wink.

He grinned. 'Not that – though we can get back to it. No, the bond. It's started to form. It's weak now, but it's there. Can't you feel it?'

I opened my mouth to say no, then closed it and

concentrated. I'd been working on blocking my awareness of Nate; perhaps I'd blocked too much. I deconstructed part of the mental wall I'd built, and warmth and loved rushed over me.

'Oh,' I said, my eyes filling up. 'It's beautiful.' It pulsed inside me like another heartbeat. And then I realised that it *was* another heartbeat: it was Emory's.

Happiness radiated from the bond, Emory's happiness. I grinned. 'This is amazing.' My bond with Emory overshadowed the accidental bond with Nate. Nate's bond was still there, but it was like a soft background tune where before it had been a roar. It was a lot more manageable.

Emory kissed me. 'Yes,' he said, 'it is. For now it's just an awareness of each other but as the bond deepens, we'll be able to tell each other's emotions and location. Some can even share the occasional thought.'

I considered that. 'Cool,' I replied.

Emory gave me a fast grin. 'I'm sorry, we'll talk more about it another time, but I've got to shower. Tom will be picking me up soon.'

'No problem.'

He got out of bed and cast a regretful look at me. I let him start the shower in the bathroom before I slunk in to join him. He had the water set to hot and steam was already pouring out. Luckily I like it hot, too. I slid open the shower door and he turned. 'I've come to wash your back,' I offered.

'Have you now?' He grinned.

'Yup. I'll help with all of those hard-to-reach areas,' I promised, falling to my knees. 'Back, crack and sac. I'll start with sac.' The water streamed over both of our bodies and we got clean while we got very, very dirty.

After our shower Emory dressed in one of his signature suits. I opened my wardrobe and found a bunch of his clothing in there. 'Is that all right?' he asked.

'I'm pretty sure that a magical bond that links us together permanently entitles you to wardrobe space.'

'If Nate gets wardrobe space too, we're going to have a problem,' Emory growled.

I laughed. 'He might have space in my house, but it's in Hes's room,' I promised.

He considered. 'I guess that's okay.'

'Thanks for your permission, your highness.' I stuck out my tongue at him.

He ignored my sarcasm. 'You're welcome, my love,' he said lightly. Then his phone rang again; Tom was on the drive. 'I've got to go.'

'Let me know how Audrey and Cuth get on,' I urged.

I saw him to the door and gave Tom a finger wave. Tom ran his eyes over my satisfied and dishevelled state, grinned broadly and gave me a thumbs up. I showed him a digit in return, but it wasn't my thumb.

I watched as they drove away before shutting the

door. Life could return to normal now, whatever that was. I called Lucy and Hes and gave them the lowdown. I saved Hes from the romantic elements of the story; they were personal, and Hes and I weren't there yet. Lucy and I discussed them in detail, and there was a lot of squealing. She was happy for me and so was her wolf, apparently. I was looking forward to meeting Esme.

I booted up my laptop and answered some emails. Emory was right: I'd been neglecting my business. After about an hour I got a text from Emory; Charlize and Catriona had both come round, and Audrey and Cuth were starting to stir. They were the last ones to have their antidote because of their ages. Relief surged through me. I'd been so sure they were going to die because Audrey had talked about it like it was a certainty. Thank goodness she wasn't a seer.

I pottered on the laptop for another hour before there was a knock on the door. I flung the door open expecting it be Emory, but it wasn't.

It was Bastion, head to toe in black and looking every inch as menacing as I knew he was. And yet, he had given me his final defence. To say my feelings were mixed would be an understatement. He had killed my parents but saved me.

He stepped into my house without waiting for an invitation, and we went into the lounge. Gato came and greeted him, and I watched while the assassin greeted him in turn. 'It's good to see you,' Bastion said.

Gato woofed and wagged his tail then gave him a lick. The barest hint of a smile tugged at the assassin's lips. 'Only you could get away with that,' he said. Gato chased his tail in excitement.

'What the fuck is going on?' The question exploded out of me; I couldn't have held it back if I had wanted to.

'It's time for your one question,' Bastion said. 'Make it the right one. I won't let you divine me again.'

I knew the question; I'd had it ready since the moment I'd met him. I let the ocean recede, and I reached closer to him to touch his skin. Who had hired him to kill my parents?

George and Mary Sharp were sitting in the living room. 'Cup of tea?' Mary offered.

'No,' Bastion said.

'Something stronger?' George suggested.

'No.'

'Just me, then.' George stood and poured himself a whisky from the drinks cabinet. He knocked it back neat.

'I'm all right, Jack,' Mary muttered. George poured her a shot, and she threw it down, grimacing slightly at the after burn.

'Why have you summoned me?' Bastion asked finally, impatience in every line of his body.

'It's very simple,' Mary said. 'We need you to kill us.'

Shock and dismay shattered me. What the hell? Why

the hell? What the fuck?

The bond between Emory and me tugged hard. Suddenly I was back in my own body and I could feel Emory's concern. He was heading back to me as fast as he could. He was in his dragon form, flying. I don't know how I knew that but I did.

Shock was roiling through me, short-circuiting my brain.

'Wrong question.' Bastion sighed and shook his head. He nodded respectfully to Gato, stood up and left, shutting the front door quietly behind him.

I stayed there, rocking back and forth. Gato was whining, but I was stuck, locked in the horror of my own mind. As I waited for Emory to find me, I felt shattered and betrayed.

I was Humpty Dumpty, and my parents had just pushed me off the wall.

I'd need help to put myself back together again.

BOOK 4 – GLIMMER OF DECEPTION

Don't panic! Book 4 is around the corner. In fact, it is available to pre-order now! Book 4 will be the last in this series, so no need to fear any cheeky hooks at the end of book 4. You're so welcome.

Acknowledgements

Thanks to my awesome husband for his unending patience and support. Thank goodness you love reading fantasy too. Thank you for always reading my work, and giving me honest feedback, even when I don't want to hear it.

Thanks to all of my cheerleaders who keep me going through thick and thin, you know who you are. Love you.

ABOUT THE AUTHOR

Heather is an urban fantasy writer and mum. She was born and raised near Windsor, which gave her the misguided impression that she was close to royalty in some way. She is not, though she once she got a letter from the Queen's lady-in-waiting.

Heather went to university in Liverpool, where she took up skydiving and met her future husband. When she's not running around after her children, she's plotting her next book and daydreaming about vampyrs, dragons and kick-ass heroines.

Heather is a book lover who grew up reading Brian Jacques and Anne McCaffrey. She loves to travel and once spent a month in Thailand. She vows to return.

Want to learn more about Heather? Subscribe to her newsletter for behind-the-scenes scoops, free bonus material and a cheeky peek into her world. Her subscribers will always get the heads-up about the best deals on her books.

Newsletter: heathergharris.com/subscribe
Follow her Facebook Page: facebook.com/Heather-G-Harris-Author-100432708741372
Instagram: instagram.com/heathergharrisauthor
Contact info: www.HeatherGHarris.com
HeatherGHarrisAuthor@gmail.com

REVIEWS

Reviews feed Heather's soul. She'd really appreciate it if you could take a few moments to review her book and say hello.

Milton Keynes UK
Ingram Content Group UK Ltd.
UKHW010706260923
429409UK00004B/280